Also by Judy Troy

Mourning Doves

West of Venus

West of Venus

Judy Troy

Random House   New York

Library of Congress Cataloging-in-Publication Data
Troy, Judy.
West of Venus / Judy Troy.
p.   cm.
ISBN 0-679-45153-6
I. Title.
PS3570.R68W47   1997
813'.54—dc21   96-49498

Random House website address: http://www.randomhouse.com

Printed in the United States of America
on acid-free paper
24689753
First Edition

For Miller Solomon

Acknowledgments

I would like to thank the Whiting Foundation; my colleagues in the Auburn University English Department, especially Dennis Rygiel; Mark Siegert; Georges and Anne Borchardt; Mary D. Kierstead, always; and Daniel Menaker, for his excellent suggestions and energetic support.

West of Venus

1

olly Parker was sitting in the front row of the viewing
room at Nyles Funeral Home, wishing she'd bribed
her son, Owen, into coming. The funeral was a disaster. The
Venus paper had gotten the time wrong, and so almost no
one had come. Holly hoped for somebody—even her ex-
husband—to walk in and occupy one of the many empty
chairs behind her.

It was Morgan Holman who had died. He'd committed
suicide. His wife, Marvelle, who was Holly's closest friend,
was sitting next to Holly, and next to Marvelle was Marvelle's
screwed-up thirty-one-year-old son, Curtis. Behind them
was the almost deserted room; outside rain was falling.
Through the window Holly could see the sad-looking dog-

woods, just past blooming, and the old army jeep Curtis had insisted on driving; his father had been a Vietnam veteran.

Morgan was probably better off dead, Holly found herself thinking. Weren't there a lot of unhappy people in the world who'd just as soon not keep living? Then, seeing her own face in the rain-streaked window, framed against the black hearse parked outside, she tried to tell herself she'd meant: I wish Morgan had been happier.

She felt better when the door opened and Marvelle's friend, Gene Rollison, walked in. He was wearing his state trooper uniform. He didn't come up to the casket, which was closed and had three wreaths of flowers on it. He sat in the middle of the fourth row with his large hands on the back of the chair in front of him. Holly smiled at him, and he waved by raising the fingers of one hand, as if it were a private signal between them.

Marvelle had not stopped crying. Her face was so wet with tears it reminded Holly of a pond reflecting back what looked into it, which was Curtis, at this moment, asking his mother something in his low, slow voice. For the first time Holly could see a real expression in his eyes—not pain, exactly, but something final slowly registering.

"Mom," he was whispering. "Didn't Dad have some savings bonds?"

At the cemetery, Holly stood in the rain next to Gene Rollison, listening to Franklin Sanders, the minister of the Venus United Methodist Church, talk about God's love. Morgan had hardly ever attended church, and Marvelle had finally stopped going, but she often mentioned Franklin. Holly had heard about Franklin's unhappy marriage; she knew that his favorite hymn was "I Need Thee Every Hour"; and she'd had explained to her the controversy over his old, faded MAKE LOVE NOT WAR T-shirt, which he wore to softball games.

Now he was reciting the Twenty-third Psalm. When he read, "He maketh me to lie down in green pastures: He leadeth me beside the still waters," he broke down himself and had to remain silent for a few seconds before he could continue.

*L*ate in the afternoon, Holly was relieved to see that people who had missed the funeral showed up at Marvelle's house, which was ten miles from Venus, out past the forest preserve, down a gravel road, and built haphazardly into a hill. Morgan had built it himself, and as Holly stood in the kitchen, slicing a coffee cake, she looked at the unfinished walls and the cigarette burns in the counter and wondered why she and everybody else who knew the Holmans hadn't seen this coming. Morgan had been an electrician, but he hadn't worked in years; if he went into town at all it was just to gas up his jeep or stop for something at the hardware store. He was polite but never talkative, and he didn't look healthy; he was unnaturally thin. And there were days, Holly remembered, when Morgan's quietness had a dangerous feeling, though not something you'd be afraid of for yourself.

Curtis, who was still living at home, was in the room the kitchen opened onto, showing his father's gun collection to

the funeral director—a Vietnam veteran himself, who sometimes hunted deer on the Holmans' property. Holly heard
Curtis say, "Dad probably would want you to have one, but
darn it, he never said that for certain."

Holly knew that the gun Morgan had shot himself with
was still at the police station. She knew this firsthand, because
Gene Rollison had told her late Friday afternoon, just two
hours after Morgan's body had been found in the willows
that grew along Black Creek. Gene had surprised her by
coming to her house, asking if he could talk to her. She'd
been fixing dinner to take to Marvelle and Curtis.

"Morgan was on his back, shot through the heart," Gene
had said, "the way you'd shoot a deer. Usually people shoot
themselves in the head."

"Maybe people shoot themselves where they hurt most,"
Holly had said.

But Morgan's suicide hadn't seemed real to her yet; what
was more upsetting was that Gene Rollison, as used to death
as he was, was sitting at her kitchen table, quietly crying. He
hadn't known Morgan at all, but he and Marvelle had been
seeing each other in secret. Holly wasn't sure for how long,
or whether or not they'd slept together. She'd never asked
Marvelle a thing about it. People needed to have a few secrets, Holly felt—mostly because she had secrets of her own.

Gene Rollison was in Marvelle's living room now, in a
chair next to the window, talking to a Venus policeman. They
both looked up when Holly came back into the room, but
then so did everyone—Holly realized she'd forgotten to take
off Marvelle's KISS THE COOK apron. She quickly untied and
removed it.

Franklin Sanders was standing by himself next to the woodstove, a tall man in his early sixties, with gray hair. "Would you like coffee?" Holly asked him.

"No, thank you," he said. "I'll probably be going in just a few minutes," although an hour later Holly saw him still standing in the same place.

It was thundering outside, and Morgan's hunting dogs were barking in response. The dogs were penned up a little distance from the house, next to the garage where Morgan had been working forever on an ancient and broken Triumph motorcycle. Holly felt a sudden flash of relief for Marvelle, and then she felt so guilty she brought a piece of cake to Nedra Holman, Morgan's senile mother. Nedra hadn't attended the funeral; Holly had picked her up afterward at the Springhaven Retirement Center and brought her here. Nedra was under the impression—of her own making—that Morgan was on his way home from Vietnam. She thought this gathering was his surprise party.

"Thanks, honey," she said now to Holly. "I could use a sweet." She was wearing a flowered dress and sitting on the edge of a threadbare chair, next to Curtis's girlfriend, Wendy Dell, who was trying to tell her that the Vietnam War had been over for twenty years.

"Give it up," Curtis said. He had come into the room and was standing behind Wendy's chair. "Grandma," he said softly. "Those guys who walked on the moon are still up there."

Marvelle was standing alone at the screen door. Even from here, Holly thought, you could tell that something awful had happened to her. She was a big woman who now looked almost fragile, like a tree you were seeing for the first time without leaves. Behind her Holly could see rain falling, filling the ruts in the driveway. Often at this time of day Holly would drive out after work, if she and Marvelle had worked the lunch shift, and the two of them would walk through the fields that Morgan had inherited from his father. They'd walk south on a crooked trail that somewhere along the way left Kansas and became Oklahoma, though where, exactly, you couldn't tell.

Wasn't that just the opposite of death, Holly thought now, looking out at the darkening afternoon—at least death as it seemed to the survivors? For the dead person, dying might not feel so final; Holly wondered if Morgan, for instance, might have felt just some subtle thing, like crossing a border into another country, or walking into a woods he'd never seen before.

She joined Marvelle at the screen door. "Did you think it was a nice funeral?" Marvelle asked her. "I mean, even though hardly anybody came?"

"It was just right," Holly said. "Morgan would have been happy with it."

"I hope so. Not that it makes one bit of difference."

Across the room, Wendy began to sing "Oh, Blessed Jesus." She sang on the radio every Saturday night, on Gussie Dell's "Neighbor Talk" program; Gussie was her mother. Wendy also sang in the Methodist choir. During the week she worked as a secretary at the middle school.

"For God's sake," Marvelle whispered, "does this look like a church to her?"

On the wall above Wendy's head was one of Morgan's posters—an almost naked young woman on a motorcycle.

The poster had depressed Holly when she and Marvelle used to exercise in this room—not just because she knew she'd never look that way but because she could imagine how hard that girl would have to work for the rest of her life in order to maintain herself.

When Wendy finished singing, the room seemed to Holly to brighten a little. She felt that people were breathing normally again. Outside, the sky had begun to clear; the rain was only a drizzle now, falling with the same slowness with which it was dripping from the trees, and there was a feeling in the house that time had suddenly speeded up. The afternoon of Morgan's funeral was over.

Holly and Marvelle went into the kitchen to look through the casserole dishes. "Almost everyone brought baked beans," Holly said. "I should have organized this so you'd get a balanced meal."

The phone rang, and Holly watched Marvelle pick up the receiver and say hello. Marvelle was standing perfectly still. "You've got to be kidding," she said finally, and hung up. "Olan Mills," Marvelle told Holly. "Selling family photographs."

She looked at the pot of beans Holly was holding. "Death isn't the worst thing that can happen to you," she said quietly. "It's worse when it happens to someone else."

"Is there any more coffee?" Gene Rollison asked as he walked up behind them.

"I'll make more," Holly told him. "It will give me something to do." She rinsed out the coffeepot while Marvelle got a carton of milk out of the refrigerator.

"I don't take milk as a rule," Gene told Marvelle.

"Oh," Marvelle said. "That's right. What was I thinking?"

"Well, you have a lot on your mind," Gene said.

Marvelle put the milk back in the refrigerator so slowly that Holly wondered if she was moving slowly on purpose, in order to concentrate longer on the ordinary, everyday things. Holly noticed that Gene was also watching Marvelle. He watched her that way—and often Holly, too—at the Hearth, the restaurant where Holly and Marvelle worked. He would sit at a booth at lunchtime with that same expression on his face. It was hard to read, Holly thought, hard to guess what he might be thinking or feeling. Now, Holly imagined, Gene was feeling love for Marvelle, even if it was tinged with guilt.

Lately, nothing seemed as important to Holly as love; she believed it was on people's minds almost all the time, and that it was what most people died feeling, one way or another. Holly thought that was even true in Morgan's case—maybe more so, in fact, though it might be a complicated kind of love that seemed to leave out everybody else. But if you were about to kill yourself, Holly felt, you were past being responsible for the people who loved you.

Marvelle and Gene had sat down at the kitchen table and were looking out the window at two deer in the ravine behind the house. "They're so pretty," Marvelle said. "Usually I only see deer when they're being field dressed, or when they're strapped to the hood of a car."

"Have you ever gone camping?" Gene asked her. "I bet you'd like it."

"I wouldn't like those tent parks," Marvelle said. "I like sleeping in a bed and having a hot shower in the morning."

"They're called campgrounds," Gene said gently.

A moment later, through the open kitchen door, Holly watched the owner of the hardware store walk into the house. There were two people she didn't know coming up the walk behind him.

"Is he here?" Nedra Holman asked. "Morgan, is that you?" she called out to a room that suddenly became completely quiet "Honey, we thought you were never coming home."

2

arly Thursday morning, two and a half weeks later, Holly dreamed that her sixteen-year-old son, Owen, was still living with her. Her first thought when she woke up was what to make him for breakfast. Outside, blue jays that had gathered around her empty feeder were chirping; she got up and put on her robe and fed them, instead.

For the past year Owen had been living with his father, Burke, and Burke's young girlfriend, Annette, at the Acres of Trailers Mobile Home Park. Owen had made that choice himself. "Dad lets me do more stuff," he had told Holly, which was certainly true. Burke didn't have rules for himself, let alone for Owen. He did things like drop firecrackers into gopher holes. Burke was why Owen now had a tattoo, she thought; it was why he was talking about quitting school; and it was why he had a dirt bike he could one day kill himself on. When Morgan Holman's suicide entered her mind a second later, she had to keep herself from driving over to Burke's right then, to make sure that Owen was all right, that he was just sitting in the kitchen having Pop-Tarts or donuts or whatever junk food it was they let him eat for breakfast.

It was late April and warm, with clouds gathering in the west over the wheat fields that were separated from Holly's backyard by Spring Ditch. She lived west of Venus, on Old Highway 73, which wasn't used much anymore except by local traffic. Holly stood in the front yard next to the bright leaves of her mulberry tree and watched a truck pull out of the lumberyard across the road. Instead of the driver losing control and smashing into her and her front porch, as Holly momentarily imagined, he waved.

Inside, Holly poured herself coffee and walked around her living room, picking up bits of newspaper Owen had overlooked the night before. He'd come over for dinner, and afterward he'd cut up the Venus paper in order to piece together some kind of note for his girlfriend—he wouldn't tell Holly what it said.

"Why can't you just talk to her?" Holly had asked him.

"I don't know," he'd told her. "I just picture a kidnapping note." Holly walked down the hall now and stood in the doorway to his old room, trying to connect the child he used to be to the criminal she was afraid he was becoming.

The phone rang, and Holly answered it in her bedroom. "It's me," Marvelle said. "I've been up since five. I did the laundry, and I went out to the garage and looked at Morgan's motorcycle. I looked at it like it was going to tell me something."

"I wish you'd take those sleeping pills the doctor gave you."

"They make it too hard for me to think," Marvelle said. Holly heard the television in the background—she guessed Curtis would have turned it on—and then Marvelle said, "A bird was trapped in the garage, not able to find its way out even when I had the door open. Then it flew into a wall and I thought, this is just like Morgan, isn't it, hurting itself when it doesn't have to."

"You need to get out of that house," Holly told her. "Meet me at the truck stop in fifteen minutes."

"Why?" Marvelle said. But then she agreed. It was now just a little before eight.

Holly dressed, locked her house, and on the way to her car waved to small, handsome Lawson Dyer, who, with his Doberman at his heels, was sweeping grass clippings off the front steps of his veterinary clinic next door. His clinic was a small white house, like Holly's, which he'd bought and remodeled the same year she had bought her house. He'd planted an apricot tree and three ornamental pear trees in front, which were flowering now.

"Don't your pear trees look pretty," Holly called out. He'd stopped sweeping and was watching her get into her car. His wife had left him two months earlier for Reese Nyles, the funeral director, and then a month later she left Reese for Rusty Fisher, a Venus policeman. Lawson had told Holly these facts one morning, two weeks ago, when he'd been trying to drag his Doberman out of her trash.

"I'm past being humiliated," he'd told her. "I think I'm just about ready to date."

Now he smiled and waved. "You can never have too many trees," he called back to her. He waved again as she started her Chevette and pulled away from the curb.

The truck stop was half the distance to Marvelle's house, just off the highway at Exit 7. Holly's father used to stop there for gas and cigarettes when she was growing up, and to buy Holly candy bars: "Because it drives your mother crazy," he'd tell Holly.

She pulled into the parking lot and into an empty space next to Marvelle's blue pickup. She walked in past Boot City, which besides cowboy boots sold denim shirts, belt buckles, and country music tapes. In the crowded restaurant Marvelle was sitting at a window booth, drinking coffee.

"I know I'm late—I'm sorry," Holly said.

"It doesn't matter," Marvelle told her. "I've just been sitting here, watching two vultures swoop down on a road kill."

Holly sat down across from her, trying not to look critically at Marvelle's unwashed hair or her stained T-shirt.

"Morgan was going to turn fifty this fall," Marvelle said. "I dreamed I bought him nicotine gum and a subscription to *Men's Health*."

"Maybe I should start spending nights with you again," Holly said. She had spent four nights at Marvelle's house following Morgan's death, sleeping next to her in the caved-in double bed that had once belonged to Franklin Sanders. Marvelle had bought it one year at the Methodist church rummage sale. It was the most uncomfortable bed Holly had ever slept in, but she wouldn't have gotten much sleep anyway; Marvelle had been up most of those four nights. She had walked around the dark house until Holly had coaxed her back to bed; she had shown Holly pictures of Morgan before he'd gone to Vietnam. Morgan had been healthier-looking back then, more hopeful-looking, maybe, but Holly didn't think he'd looked all that happy. She hadn't known if she should tell Marvelle that or not.

"I have to get used to being by myself," Marvelle said now. She was looking at something out the window, and Holly saw a state-police car pulling up. Gene Rollison, in his uniform— a starched blue shirt and gray pants—got out and walked toward the door. Holly watched him remove his hat and smooth down his light hair.

"You don't mind if he sits with us, do you?" Holly asked, and when Gene walked in she waved him over before Marvelle had a chance to answer. But first he was waylaid by a county judge, and then by Gussie Dell, one booth over, who was sitting with her sister.

"Where do they find that nice shade of blue?" Gussie Dell said loudly. "And why do they waste it on a uniform that scares the hell out of people?"

"Don't listen to her," Gussie's sister told Gene. "It doesn't scare me."

"That's because you're not a criminal like your sister," Gene told her.

"I wasn't speeding," Gussie said. "I said it then and I'll say it now. Meanwhile, you're going to sterilize yourself with that radar gun."

Holly could see Gene blushing. "Gene Rollison," she called out. "Come and sit with me. I need to ask you something."

"Go ahead," Gussie told him, as he made his way to Holly's booth. "Why spend time with old people like us?"

Holly slid over in the booth, and Gene sat down beside her. "I have one question," Holly said. "I want to know how soon in life you can tell if somebody's going to become a *real* criminal."

"What do you mean by real?" Gene asked.

"Not like Gussie Dell," Holly said. "Somebody you'd hate to be the mother of."

Gene looked thoughtful. "Fourth grade," he said. "Last year, I talked to a fourth-grade class in Ferrisville."

The waitress, an older, heavyset woman named Leona who had worked at the truck stop for as long as Holly could remember, brought Gene and Holly coffee and took their orders. Marvelle only asked for toast. "What did those children do?" Holly asked Gene, after Leona had walked away.

"They shot spitballs at me," Gene said. "Right at my head," he told Holly and Marvelle when he caught them exchanging glances. "All right," he said then. "It's not what you send people to prison for. But they interrupted my safety film."

Outside the day had turned dark. Without Holly noticing, clouds had moved in and the wind had increased; she could see the long grasses in the ditch along the highway being blown almost flat.

"My clothes are out on the line, and I left my windows open," Marvelle said. "Curtis isn't home. He left when I did, to help Wendy Dell start her car."

"I'll go," Gene said. He was already on his feet. "It will take me just a few minutes to get out there and close things up."

"I can't ask you to do that," Marvelle said, just as rain began to blow almost horizontally past the window.

"I know. That's why I'm offering." He picked up Marvelle's keys, which were on the table next to her coffee cup, and Holly and Marvelle watched him leave the restaurant and run through the rain to his car. A moment later he was speeding out of the parking lot.

"I should have said no," Marvelle told Holly. "I don't want anything to do with him anymore. I've already told him that."

"He wanted to help," Holly said. "He's a nice person. You can't expect him to become another person."

"Did we lose someone?" Leona asked, serving their breakfasts. The question startled both of them; Holly could see that Marvelle had thought just what she had, for a second—that Leona had meant Morgan.

"Gene will be right back," Holly explained. "We'll order him a fresh breakfast then."

Outside, the wind had died down but rain was falling hard. Holly watched Leona bring coffee to three truck drivers sitting at the counter, in the smoking section. That was where Holly's ex-husband, Burke, had always liked to sit. He'd wanted to be mistaken for a truck driver. "For somebody employed," Holly had finally said to him out loud, instead of to herself, which was the beginning of the end of their marriage.

"Can you imagine all the conversations Leona has heard?" Holly asked Marvelle. "She once heard Burke say, 'I could be as famous as Elvis if I'd had Elvis's opportunities.' "

"Morgan used to stop in here back when he had that army friend," Marvelle said. "They liked to eat here late at night when there was nothing going by on the highway but trucks."

"I wonder what they talked about," Holly said.

"UFO's, probably. They wanted to go to other planets." Marvelle looked down at Gene's cold breakfast. "I don't know what they talked about in private. Maybe they talked about me." A tear rolled down her face and onto the table. She ignored it and ate her toast.

Half an hour later, Gene Rollison pulled back into the parking lot, the steadily falling rain illuminated in his headlights. When he came into the restaurant and sat down beside Holly, he was so wet she thought she could feel the dampness in her own clothes.

"I wiped up your floors," he told Marvelle, handing her the keys, "and I put your wet laundry in the bathtub."

"Thanks." Marvelle stood up and motioned to Leona for Gene's breakfast. Then she walked quickly toward the rest room.

"What did I do wrong?" Gene asked Holly.

"It's not you," Holly told him. "We were talking about Morgan."

She watched him put his hat on the table and drink his cold coffee. Gene's hair was light brown, his eyes green, and he had large, uneven features. He was good-looking in an unexpected way; Holly didn't realize it at first, but she'd find herself paying more attention each time she saw him. Marvelle had introduced Holly to Gene a year and a half ago at the Hearth, but Holly had already known who he was. The judge who spoke to Gene when he entered the truck stop had once tried to draft him to run for county sheriff.

"I'd sooner run from here to the Pacific Ocean," Gene was quoted in the paper as saying.

And Holly had met Gene in person even before that, back when she was still married. She'd been at a gas station in Ferrisville one afternoon, struggling with her oil cap, when she looked up to see a tall, big-shouldered policeman offering to help. "My husband was supposed to do this," Holly had told Gene.

Gene had surprised her by saying, "You deserve better than that."

Holly wasn't sure if Gene even remembered.

Now, as the judge stopped at their booth to discuss the Venus High School baseball team, Holly looked at Gene's interesting face and listened to him talk about how half the team was ineligible due to failing grades.

"That could have happened to my son, Owen," Holly said, after the judge walked away.

"Does he play baseball?" Gene asked.

"No," Holly told him. "He just gets bad grades."

She and Gene were quiet then, waiting for Marvelle. Their eyes met and they both awkwardly looked away. Holly watched Gussie Dell's sister, Beatrice Keel, comb her sparse hair. Beatrice had had cancer; Gussie had talked about it on "Neighbor Talk." Holly remembered Gussie once saying, "My sister's doctor comes and goes so fast he might as well walk into her room backwards."

When Marvelle returned from the rest room, she leaned across the table and said softly to Holly and Gene, "Gussie Dell's earring fell in the toilet. She's trying to fish it out."

A few minutes later, Gussie came out of the rest room with her hand raised. "Here it is," she shouted to her sister, who picked up a menu and hid behind it.

"I washed it off real well," Gussie told the restaurant at large.

Leona brought Gene's breakfast, which he ate quickly, in addition to eating the bacon and toast from his original breakfast. "Don't you ever eat?" Holly asked him.

"I'm not a very good cook," he said.

The three of them smiled and then sat silently. The rain had stopped. Holly watched two crows fly across the highway into the branches of an oak tree.

What did Morgan see the morning he walked out with his gun across the fields to Black Creek, she found herself wondering. It had been a bright day, she remembered; at this time of year there was usually a crane or a heron flying over the creek, and grackles singing in the sweet gum trees. Holly imagined that if she were walking across those fields, she'd think about the birds—what their mating habits were and where their nests might be. Then she would probably think about some aspect of her own life. She couldn't stop wondering what Morgan had been thinking, walking away from his family and himself. After he died, she thought, whatever birds had flown away at the sound of his gunshot probably flew back again, and went on singing.

3

Late that afternoon Holly drove to the Hearth in her yellow Chevette to work the dinner shift. The Hearth was not a big restaurant; there were eight red booths and ten tables, and a fireplace in the back corner that had never drawn right. The cook, Cleveland Harris, offered specials each night. Tonight's was liver and onions, with blackberry cobbler for dessert, and Holly could smell the onions cooking as she set the tables in the front half of the restaurant.

Will Chaffe, who owned the Hearth, was on the phone at the counter, where the cash register was. Holly overheard him say, "Why do you always pick fights with me when I'm at work?" and then, "I don't know why you're not happier, Evelyn. I've never known why."

Holly put four water glasses on a window table and tried not to look in Will's direction. A year ago, just after Owen moved out, she and Will had had an affair, which Holly had ended three months ago. She'd never told anyone about it, not even Marvelle. Will had asked her not to, and Holly was glad; secrecy had made things more exciting. She'd meet Will in the walk-in cooler, for example, where he would put his hands under her uniform while Marvelle or Cleveland would be standing just outside the door. And once, in the middle of a slow Saturday night, he'd completely undressed her in the storeroom. For a few minutes she'd been standing in front of the canned goods, naked.

Now, as Holly pretended not to listen to Will's conversation, she looked out the window at a teenage couple embracing. It was four-thirty. The day had turned cool, after the rain, more like March than late April, and Holly could see flyers of some kind being scattered by the wind up and down the wet street.

"I guess you heard that," Will said to Holly, after he got off the phone. He walked over to the table she was setting and sank down in one of the chairs.

"I wouldn't have come in here if I'd known you were talking to her," Holly said.

"I'm glad you heard. You can see that my life is just the way it always was, except that now I don't have you."

"Don't make me apologize again," Holly told him. "It's not fair. I don't know what I'm apologizing for."

"For not loving me anymore," Will said quietly.

Marvelle walked in then, carrying a tray full of silverware, and Will went into the kitchen. Holly didn't know what she would have said next. She wished he would stop talking about love; as important as she thought love was, it made her nervous. All she knew was that if she weren't able to have contact with Will at work—even just to exchange glances with him across the room—she would probably still be having an affair with him. She would still be standing alone at her front door, watching him get into his car to drive home to his wife and four children.

"Does Will think it's going to be busy tonight?" Marvelle asked. "Is he remembering it's bingo night across the street?"

"He must know," Holly said, "but he didn't say anything."

"Cleveland thinks Will is unhappy," Marvelle said.

"Well, a lot of people are unhappy," Holly told her impatiently. "Probably most of the world is unhappy."

They distributed the silverware and put on each table one of the red candles they used at night, then lit them. Most aspects of being a waitress had become old to Holly—if she'd been smart enough to not get pregnant and have to marry Burke, she would have gone to community college or some kind of technical school—but she still liked this moment when the restaurant was empty and candlelit and smelled like cooking. It reminded her of the life she hoped she was getting into when she got married, which, though it hadn't panned out, still existed here in feeling, anyway, for these few minutes before people started coming in and wanting things.

*L*awson Dyer was Holly's first customer. He said he'd closed the veterinary clinic early and spent the afternoon finally getting rid of every pink thing his wife had left in the house. "I meant to do it right after she left, but it was hard," he told Holly. "Even curtains remind you of something. But it feels good not to see that color." Holly looked down at her pink uniform. "Now, I don't always mind pink," Lawson said quickly. "It's becoming on you."

"Will Chaffe's wife makes us wear these," Holly said. "She has terrible taste."

She handed Lawson a menu and walked over to Marvelle, who was standing next to the fireplace. The funeral director, Reese Nyles, and a date were sitting down in her section.

"I can't stand to see him," Marvelle told Holly. "I look at him and think about Morgan's funeral."

"I'll wait on Reese if you take care of Lawson Dyer."

Holly had known Reese Nyles since the eighth grade; his family had lived across the street from Burke's family. He was seven years older than Holly. She could remember him coming home once, on leave, before he left for Vietnam. He'd seemed foreign and interesting with his short hair and serious expression; she remembered looking at him and thinking: He might never be coming back.

Now she walked over and heard him say, "No one thinks of undertaking as an ordinary profession. People think I'm some kind of vampire." Reese was dressed in black jeans and a black shirt, his collar-length hair slicked back, the lit candle on the table reflecting weirdly in his thick glasses.

"The special is liver and onions," Holly said, handing them menus.

"Oh my God," the date said, and then, looking at the menu, "I haven't seen this kind of food since before I moved up to Kansas City."

"So I guess you don't like liver?" Reese asked her.

"It makes me sick to even smell it," she said.

"Two specials," Reese said to Holly, as a joke.

"I'll give you a few minutes to make a real decision," Holly told him. She brought menus to a family sitting at a booth and, because Marvelle was in the kitchen, poured water for a big, balding man who had sat down with Lawson. Then she returned to Reese, who was watching his date shine up the silverware with her napkin.

"We'll both try the broiled chicken," Reese said. "Do you recommend that, Holly?"

"Everything Cleveland makes is good," Holly said.

"Could I have my salad dressing on the side?" his date asked. "I want the low-fat kind. Also, I like my chicken without the skin."

"You don't mind if they leave the head on, though, do you?" Reese asked her.

Holly had another customer waving her over, or she would have tried to hear the answer. One thing she still liked about waitressing was the way you became invisible to people. They said whatever they felt like in front of you.

She was so busy for the next hour and a half that she was surprised, when things slowed down, to realize that it was night and that the streetlights had come on. Later, after the last customer left, she and Marvelle went out front and stood on the dark sidewalk. They watched cars leaving the parking lot of the Catholic church across the street.

"Cleveland's wife won a hundred dollars at bingo last week," Marvelle said.

"Gussie Dell announced that on 'Neighbor Talk,' " Holly told her. " 'Why don't we have bingo at the Methodist church?' she said. 'Does Franklin Sanders expect us to fork over money forever without winning any of it back?' "

"She embarrasses Franklin," Marvelle said. "He's always afraid of what she's going to say next."

"I don't blame him," Holly said.

She was looking at Will's car, a red Buick with a dent in the side, which was parked in front of the restaurant. She looked at the MY CHILD IS A STUDENT AT VENUS ELEMENTARY bumper sticker and at the plastic dinosaurs in the back window. There were coloring books on the backseat floor, Holly remembered, and a rubber snake in the glove compartment. She'd watched a talk show one afternoon about the end of love affairs, in which a woman had said, "I'll cry just seeing a car like his." Holly had never felt that way about anyone. That comment had only made her think of Morgan, who had sometimes cried at nothing, or what seemed like nothing. The things that mattered most to people might be invisible to everybody else, Holly thought, maybe even to the people themselves.

"You know that man who sat down with Lawson Dyer?" Marvelle said as she and Holly went back into the Hearth. "He left a big tip and complimented the food."

"He must be from out of town," Holly said.

She started to clear her tables. She did it slowly, because Will had come in to help. She liked looking at his dark hair and his ironed shirt and the concentrated look on his face as he picked up plates, glasses, and silverware. He was conscientious no matter what he did—too conscientious making love, Holly had thought, when he'd tried too hard to kiss her as deeply as she liked, or to bite the back of her neck softly, as she'd once asked him to, or to move his hand very slowly down along her spine, which she told him felt sexy. He'd worked so hard that Holly sometimes felt like a road map he was trying to read.

But the afternoon she remembered most was completely different. It was the last time they were together, when Will had stopped her in the hallway outside her bedroom and greedily undressed her while he undid his belt and unzipped his pants. He'd apologized for it afterward, and Holly had said, "Sex should make you carried away like that. Otherwise, you might as well be married."

As soon as she'd said it, even before she saw the troubled look on Will's face, she knew that she'd revealed a bad thing about herself. "You're too cynical," her mother had told her more than once, and Holly could almost see the truth of it, which was that she didn't trust men, and she didn't trust love, and she wasn't about to have sex with someone she cared for too much.

After Will left that afternoon, going home as usual to his wife and children—who had never seemed quite real to Holly, even when she saw them in the restaurant—she took a shower and changed the sheets on her bed, and the next day she told Will she couldn't be with him anymore.

"I feel too guilty," she had said, but the truth was she felt uncomfortable around him now that he knew something so personal about her. She didn't feel as sexy as she had before. The idea of going to bed with someone who really knew you, who you didn't want to live without—Holly couldn't imagine it. That would be like standing up in a roller coaster, she thought, or like opening the door in an airborne plane. But lately, now that she wasn't sleeping with Will, she'd started feeling attracted to him again.

"What are you looking so secretive about?" he asked her now, in the dining room, as Marvelle went off to the kitchen with a big tray of dirty dishes.

"I was just remembering a certain afternoon," Holly said flirtatiously.

"Why are you driving me crazy?" Will said to her.

A little before nine, after Marvelle had gone home and Holly had just finished setting her tables for breakfast, Gene Rollison walked in and asked if it was too late for him to have coffee and dessert. Will sat him in a booth. Gene was out of uniform, wearing a plaid shirt, jeans, and a black wind-breaker, which Holly especially noticed because of the snug way it fit his shoulders. She brought him coffee and black-berry cobbler.

"Has Rusty Fisher been in tonight?" Gene asked. "I couldn't get him at home. I wanted to ask him about these." Gene reached into his pocket and brought out three of the flyers Holly had seen blowing around in the street earlier. They were creased and dirty, and it took Holly a minute to realize that they were photocopies of Owen's message to his girlfriend, which turned out to be NOT HAVING SEX CAN KILL YOU. Holly recognized the NOT and the CAN and the YOU.

"What they say is bad enough," Gene said, "since it sounds like some kind of death threat, but the fact that we're close to the state line, plus the fact that the perpetrator avoided handwriting or even a computer, makes me wonder if we shouldn't get the FBI involved."

"The perpetrator?" Holly said, sitting down across from him. "The perpetrator is my son, Owen. He put that message together as a joke for his girlfriend. I don't know how it got Xeroxed or out in the street. Maybe he thought that would be funny, too. He has his father's sense of humor."

Gene frowned at Holly, put the copies back in his pocket, and picked up his fork. "You and I will go out and get rid of as many of these we can find," he told her.

"Good," Holly said. "Thank you." She paid for his dessert herself.

*H*olly and Gene drove up and down Venus Avenue, picking up copies of Owen's handiwork, and then down Oak and Hyacinth and Beech, finding strays that had blown up against fences or lay flattened in gutters. If it hadn't been for the bright moon illuminating the white paper, Holly didn't know how she and Gene would have seen them. There weren't as many as she had imagined, and she felt disappointed—looking for the flyers made her feel almost close to Owen. It wasn't very often that you could be helpful to a teenage child, she thought, except for giving him money. And Gene's earnestness was making her feel that she was keeping Owen out of jail.

"This could have been a serious situation," he said as they retrieved flyers from the lawn of the Venus Baptist Church. "A death threat is no laughing matter."

"I know that," Holly said. "I worry about what's going to happen to him. But it's not really a death threat. Don't you think it's even a little funny?"

"Well, no. I don't." They got into his car. "But I don't have the best sense of humor," he admitted. "I don't always get jokes. Although I think I can make them."

"That's something to be thankful for," Holly said.

Afraid she'd been sarcastic, she began to ask Gene questions about himself. He told her about growing up on a ranch in western Nebraska and never again wanting to ride a horse, and about how he'd married at eighteen and gotten divorced five years later. He had a sister who owned a garden center in Omaha, and a survivalist brother who was a geologist in Montana.

And finally he told her about how he'd felt finding Morgan's body in the willows along Black Creek. By this time he and Holly were done collecting the flyers and he had invited her out to his mobile home. They were in his backyard, burning the flyers in a big trash barrel. Gene lived north of the high school, just inside the county line, on a hill from which you could see the lights of Ferrisville. He didn't have neighbors, just fields sloping down from either side of the acre of land he owned, which, Holly could see in the moonlight, was mowed in circles.

"It's not like I'd never seen a dead body before," he told her. "But knowing that it was Marvelle's husband, well, I still can't get it out of my mind."

"I can imagine," Holly said. "But wasn't there a secret part of you that felt hopeful?"

"No," Gene said. "I don't think so."

They went inside once the fire was out. Gene's trailer was larger and neater than Holly had expected. She sat on his brown couch while he went into the kitchen to make hot chocolate, and she looked at the framed pictures of his family, which he had lined up, in order of frame size, on his coffee table. It seemed to Holly that everyone in the family was looking at the camera in the same way—with that decent, well-meaning expression Gene often had. She could picture every one of them showing safety films to nine-year-olds.

"Your family is very wholesome-looking," she said to Gene when he brought in the hot chocolate.

"Thank you." He gave her a napkin and sat in a chair that matched the couch.

"I don't mean wholesome as in foolish," Holly said.

"I didn't think you did," Gene told her. "I didn't think that after I helped keep Owen out of trouble you'd say something insulting to me." He smiled at Holly, and she hesitantly smiled back.

"Speaking of Owen," she said then, to change the subject, "I'm not sure what to say to him. Maybe I should tell him the FBI came to talk to me."

"I don't think I'd lie," Gene said. "Not about this, anyway. I mean, some things are worth lying about and some things aren't."

"No kidding," Holly said.

"Was Will Chaffe worth lying about?" Gene asked quickly.

Holly spilled a little of her hot chocolate.

"I don't think it's general knowledge," he told her. "I was just paying attention."

They left soon after, Gene driving Holly back to the Hearth to pick up her car. The night had gotten colder, and Holly huddled in her jacket.

"Will Chaffe is none of my business," Gene said when they were on the dark highway. "It's just that I can sense things with certain people. With some people more than with others."

"Do you always feel like you have to tell them?" Holly asked.

"No. I just feel that way with you."

Holly looked at Gene, who was careful to keep his eyes straight ahead, on the road.

"I guess I'm the same way," Holly said slowly, "about sensing things."

"What do you sense about me?" Gene asked.

Holly was silent. They passed a church, a cemetery, and a county road that wound through wheat fields and the forest preserve before it eventually led to Marvelle's house.

"I don't know how to answer that," Holly said. "I don't know what answer you're looking for."

"I want to know your answer," Gene told her.

"That's not fair," Holly said. "You're asking me to say what's in your mind before you say it."

"No I'm not," Gene told her. "I was wondering what was in your mind. I wasn't thinking about fair or unfair."

"I can see that," Holly said irritably.

She wouldn't look at Gene. She wasn't sure how their conversation had turned into an argument, although she was pretty sure it wasn't her fault.

Gene drove into town down Venus Avenue and pulled into the parking area behind the Hearth. It was empty except for Holly's small car. "I'll wait until you get your lights on," he told her.

"You don't have to."

"How about if I want to?" Gene said. "Would that be all right?"

"That would be nice," Holly said stiffly.

The engine was running and the heater was on; otherwise the only sound was Holly dropping her keys. She and Gene both bent down to pick them up, and for a moment he was leaning against her, his windbreaker slippery against the fabric of her jacket.

"Good night," he said quietly.

"Thanks for your help," Holly told him. And she got out of his warm car and into her cold one.

4

The man at the Hearth who had left Marvelle a nice tip was a friend of Lawson Dyer's from Iowa—a big, good looking, balding man named Dick Spearman. Holly and Marvelle met him three weeks later, on a Saturday morning when they were planting petunias in a section of Holly's front yard that Owen, for a new ear hole and two CD's, had dug up for Holly the week before. Dick Spearman was next door at Lawson's clinic—Holly had seen the two of them earlier, looking up at Lawson's new gutters. Then Lawson brought Dick over and introduced him.

"We've known each other how long?" Lawson said to Dick.

"I don't want to give away how old I am," Dick said.

"You couldn't possibly be any older than I am," Marvelle told him.

"I'm fifty-three," Dick said.

"Oh." Marvelle picked up her spade. "Well, it's always a mistake to say that something's impossible."

"So how old are you?" Dick asked her. "Now, don't tell me if you don't want to."

"Okay. I don't want to." Marvelle reattached one of her overall straps. Underneath she was wearing an undershirt that had once been white. Summer was still more than three weeks away, but the days were already hot. Both Marvelle and Holly were wearing Venus Seed 'n Feed visors they'd bought that morning. Marvelle's yellow visor, Holly thought, combined with her wild red hair, made her look as if she could be the mother of one of the MTV women tacked up on Owen's wall.

"Dick's staying at my place tonight," Lawson said. "Tomorrow he heads for a hog farm outside Wichita, and then up to Topeka."

"I'm a hog-sperm salesman," Dick explained.

"What do you really do?" Marvelle asked him.

"I sell hog sperm," he told her.

In the small silence that followed, Lawson squatted down next to Holly. "We wondered if you two would like to drive down to Tulsa tonight for dinner."

Holly looked over at Marvelle, who shook her head no.

"Sure," Holly said. "We'll be ready at six."

*A*fter Lawson and Dick left, getting into Lawson's Cherokee, Marvelle said to Holly, "You don't listen to me. My feelings aren't important to you."

"That's not true," Holly said. "Well, not completely." She looked at Marvelle's overalls. "Do you have anything nice to wear?"

Marvelle got up and walked over to Holly's mimosa tree in the middle of the front yard. Holly couldn't see her face, but she was pretty sure she knew how Marvelle felt, or at least how she herself would feel, if she were Marvelle: as if going out for dinner, or putting on nice clothes, or doing just about anything was hardly worth the effort.

"It's just dinner in Tulsa," Holly said. "You still have to eat, Marvelle. And you can't stay at home forever, wishing things were different. You're not dead yourself."

"I didn't say I wanted to be dead."

"Isn't that how you feel?"

"No," Marvelle said. "But the last thing I want to do is be around other men."

"It's not 'other' anymore," Holly said gently.

Marvelle didn't respond, and Holly returned to her flowers. As she planted petunias she could see in her mind, the week before Morgan's death, the tulips and daffodils blooming, and the dogwood trees; she remembered that the day of Morgan's funeral, when she'd driven Morgan's mother out to Marvelle's house, Nedra had asked her to stop, even though it was raining, so that she could pick branches from the blooming forsythia that lined the gravel road.

The world stayed the same no matter what happened to individual people, Holly was about to tell Marvelle, to comfort her. But Holly couldn't even say it. It depressed her too much. Weren't people more important than that, and shouldn't they make more of a difference? If she, for example, were to die, would Will even close up the Hearth for a day? Death was just too hard to think about, Holly decided. It was like love; it changed everything you thought into something you felt.

"Maybe we shouldn't go tonight," Holly said gloomily. "I'm not really in the mood anymore."

"I hate that you always do that," Marvelle said. "You're cheerful one minute and sad the next, and you're not all that cheerful to start with."

"That's because I think a lot. I'm a thoughtful person."

"You give thinking a bad name." Marvelle crossed the front yard and walked up to Holly's porch. "Anyway, I'm hungry, and you've already got me thinking about what to wear."

"What are you going to wear?" Holly asked.

"I don't know. I don't have anything nice. Would you go to the Ferrisville Mall with me?"

"Only if you comb your hair first," Holly said.

*T*hey went in Holly's Chevette. They drove past the Hearth, the grade school, and the park, with its little gazebo and blooming trees, and got to the intersection of Venus Avenue and Oak just in time to see Owen, in his father's truck, speed through a yellow light. "I don't know how many times I've told him not to do that," Holly said.

"Curtis drove the same way at Owen's age," Marvelle told her.

"Why don't I find that reassuring?" Holly responded.

She turned onto Ferrisville Road, which once outside of Venus became the two-lane highway Gene Rollison lived on. "Do you want to stop by Gene's, just to see him?" Holly asked. "Just to be friendly and say hello?"

"No," Marvelle said. "Not for my sake, anyway. I don't know how you can even ask that."

Holly drove on past and changed the subject to Beatrice Keel's husband—Gussie Dell's brother-in-law—whom she had seen the day before carrying a cat into Lawson's clinic. Holly had known Mr. Keel when she was a child; he and her father had bowled together on Saturday nights. More recently, however, she knew about him from listening to Gussie Dell's "Neighbor Talk" program. Gussie said that for years now, her brother-in-law had been sitting out in his chicken shed, watching television. "I'd like to dynamite him out of there," she often said.

"Even if he doesn't recognize me," Holly said to Marvelle, "he could still be friendly. Yesterday, for example, he just turned away when I said hello."

"Why does Beatrice stay with him?" Marvelle asked.

"I don't know," Holly said. "Why did I stay with Burke so long? Why did you stay with Morgan?" She said it automatically, since back when Morgan was alive she and Marvelle had asked these questions of each other probably a hundred times in the years they had been friends.

Within a second Holly was apologizing, but it was too late. Marvelle had already taken the question to heart. She was already crying.

"I don't know why I stayed," she told Holly. "I should have left him a long time ago, so that he could have found somebody who really loved him, and didn't just feel sorry for him."

Holly pulled off the highway onto a dirt road and got Marvelle Kleenex from the glove compartment. "You did love Morgan," she told her. "You took care of him and worried about him, even though he made you miserable."

Marvelle grew quiet. She was looking out the window at a hawk circling above a cottonwood tree. "You think that's love?" she asked Holly. "Then maybe that bird is going to fly down here and drive us to Ferrisville." She put her head back against the seat.

"It might be a different kind of love than you mean," Holly said defensively.

The car was hot; she opened the door, letting in a warm breeze and the smell of manure and cut grass. The dirt road she'd pulled off on led to a farmhouse, she guessed, though all she could see from here was the back of a barn, and cows lying in the shade of an oak tree. She wondered what that farmhouse looked like; she wondered if the people who lived there were happy and, if they were, how they managed it.

Marvelle blew her nose, dried her face, and said, "Let's go. We're not going to cheer ourselves up sitting here."

Holly closed the door and backed down the dirt road.

*H*alf an hour later they were parking at the back of the crowded mall parking lot. The mall in Ferrisville was just a few years old; the trees planted at the end of the parking rows were still saplings, and across the highway was a cornfield a drunken Burke had once driven Holly through in his old Mustang.

Holly and Marvelle walked into the mall past Arcade Heaven and Hair for Stars, down to Penney's, where they went to the women's department and looked through racks of dresses. Marvelle chose one to try on; it was reduced for special clearance and was in the larger size she used to wear. Holly talked her into also trying on a smaller-sized, close-fitting yellow dress.

"It won't look good on me," Marvelle said. "I look better in shapeless things."

"Maybe we should see what they have in the maternity section," Holly said sarcastically.

"That's a great idea," Marvelle said.

"It's a joke." Holly went into the dressing room next to Marvelle's and tried on a short white dress with spaghetti straps crisscrossing in the back. She was smaller than Marvelle, brown-eyed, and had short dark hair she was letting grow longer. Lately she'd gained a little weight. She stepped out into the hall and looked at herself in the three-way mirror. "What do you think?" she asked Marvelle.

"Lose ten pounds and get a suntan," Marvelle said. Then she looked at her own reflection. She was wearing the long, roomy, mouse-colored shift she'd chosen. "Isn't this nice?" she asked Holly.

"It makes me mad to hear you say that," Holly said. "You're not even trying." She was upset suddenly, and she went into the dressing room and changed back into her own clothes, leaving on the floor the dress that made her look fat and pale.

"All right," Marvelle said a few minutes later, when she tried on the dress Holly liked. "I'll get this one."

"Good," Holly said. "Thank goodness one of us will look worth taking out."

After Marvelle bought a matching pair of shoes, they walked down to the food court and ordered chicken chow mein and Cokes from China King. They sat at a table under the skylight.

"This guy had on like a Deadhead T-shirt and totally tight jeans?" they heard a teenaged girl say at a table behind them. "And when he asked me what time it was, I was like."

"God," the girl across from her said. "I would have been like."

"I know," the first girl said.

"I feel old," Holly told Marvelle. "I don't understand what kids say anymore, and I don't know how to talk to Owen, and I'm never again going to fit into a size-eight dress."

"Will you forget that dress?" Marvelle said. She picked a piece of fat out of her chow mein.

Holly was looking around at the people in the food court. Most of them were Owen's age. Even the kids with tattoos had only three ear holes, at most, Holly noticed; Owen had five. And she didn't see anyone with the kind of scowl Owen had on his face, though a few days earlier she had seen him smiling. Getting out of her car in front of the hardware store, she had seen Owen standing in the doorway of Adventure Video, where he worked part-time, talking to his former sixth-grade teacher. He had had an open, friendly expression

43

on his face, and for a moment Holly had found herself thinking what a nice person he might be.

"Oh, no," Marvelle said. "Look." She was pointing to a table near the window, where Holly saw Wendy Dell sitting with a man who wasn't Curtis, eating something off his plate.

"Maybe it's her brother," Holly said.

"She doesn't have a brother."

"How about somebody from church? Does Franklin Sanders have an assistant?"

"Would you eat food from your minister's plate, if you had a minister?"

"Well, no," Holly said. "I suppose not."

*T*hey finished their lunches and walked out into the bright, hot afternoon. The winter that year had been long and cold. At the beginning of March, when the worst of the cold seemed to be over, an ice storm had stranded Holly at Marvelle's house for twenty-four hours. She, Marvelle, and Curtis had played Clue all afternoon and evening in front of the woodstove, by candlelight. Morgan was out in the garage, tinkering with his motorcycle. Holly didn't see him until midnight, when he came inside in his dirty coveralls and army field jacket and sat with them to eat a bologna sandwich.

"You look frozen," Marvelle had said. "Take off your boots." A moment later he fell asleep in his chair with the uneaten sandwich on his knee.

Holly remembered thinking Morgan hardly seemed human anymore, but not thinking more about it. It was just how things were with Morgan.

Now Holly and Marvelle drove back to Venus on Ferris-ville Road, but this time Holly didn't say anything when they passed Gene's mobile home, even though she saw Gene out-side on his riding lawn mower, not wearing a shirt, his wide shoulders sunburned. Holly forced herself not to look. They passed the high school, and the middle school, where Wendy Dell worked, and Holly said, "You don't even like Wendy."

"That's true," Marvelle said. "I don't. But that doesn't mean I want to see Curtis hurt. He hasn't done anything to deserve that."

Well, he exists, were the words that went through Holly's mind, and she thought, maybe I should start going to church to become a nicer person. Although she couldn't see how at-tending church would change the kind of person Curtis was—unless, possibly, he went.

"There's probably some simple explanation for what we saw," she reassured Marvelle.

"That's what I'm afraid of," Marvelle said.

*A*t home, after Marvelle left, Holly swept the kitchen floor and dusted her living room. She kept busy because now, alone with her thoughts, she kept picturing Owen speeding through that intersection and probably not wearing his seat belt. She found herself imagining Gene Rollison coming over to tell her Owen had had an accident—what words he'd use and how he'd try to comfort her—and finally she dropped her dust rag on the couch, picked up the phone, and dialed Burke's number.

Burke's girlfriend, Annette, answered. "Owen's out riding his dirt bike," she told Holly.

"Is he wearing his helmet?" Holly asked.

"I don't know," Annette said. "Hold on." Holly heard her ask Burke. "We didn't notice," Annette told Holly. "We've both been real busy."

Holly asked to speak to Burke. "I don't care how busy you are," she told him. "When Owen was a baby, was I too busy to make sure he wasn't falling down the stairs, or getting into the Drano?"

"How should I know?" Burke said.

"Well, start paying attention to things," Holly told him. "Make Owen's head your first assignment."

After she hung up, she filled her bathtub, undressed, and turned on the portable radio in the bathroom. Her mother used to have a radio in her bathroom that was plugged into an outlet above the counter. "Get rid of that," Holly had told her, "or put it in another room. It's dangerous."

"I only use it when I'm across the room, in the tub," her mother had explained.

"What if a criminal broke into the house while you were bathing?" Holly had said. "What would keep him from throwing it into the bathtub with you?"

Her mother told her she was being paranoid, but now her mother lived in Wichita with Holly's stepfather, Newlin, who was even more safety-conscious than Holly was. For Christmas he bought Holly things like rug grips.

Holly's reckless father, who'd died four years earlier, had been at the other extreme. He'd lost his driver's license twice, speeding too many times down the highway in his old Camaro, and he smoked until the day he died, of heart disease, at fifty-four. "What am I supposed to do, honey?" he'd asked Holly three months before he died. "Live like I'm already dead?"

"Take care of yourself for me and Mom and Owen," she'd told him.

"That kind of leaves out number one," he'd said to Holly.

Now, in her bathtub, listening to the news on the radio, Holly reminded herself that in other parts of the world people were getting shot, or starving to death, or digging themselves out of an earthquake, while she was just quietly and safely taking a bath in her own house. The worst thing she could imagine happening was that a tornado would collapse her roof and trap her in the bathtub, and that a few hours later Gene Rollison—if she were lucky—would discover her naked.

Holly washed her hair; she dressed and put on makeup. Then she went outside and stood on her front porch and waited for Marvelle, who'd promised to be back by five-thirty. The air was cooler now. There were juncos flying into her mulberry tree. Holly couldn't get over spring, especially after such a bad winter—the way the trees became greener than you'd remembered them, and the air softer.

"Why didn't Morgan choose winter to kill himself?" Marvelle had said recently at the Hearth, on a warm night after the customers had gone; she, Holly, and Will were outside, seeing if the second H in THE HEARTH was still flickering.

"Wasn't there a poem written about that?" Will had said, and Holly had remembered the lines, too, a little, from high school, at least the memory and desire part, and how winter kept your roots unstirred. Now, as she looked at her flowers, she decided that anything beautiful was just an inch away from sad. It made you feel too much, for one thing, and reminded you that you'd never be that beautiful, yourself, even inside, because how could you change the self you were born with?

Marvelle drove up then, in her little blue pickup; she had on her new dress and her new high heels, and she was smiling as she got out, pointing to a ruby-throated hummingbird that had just flown up to Holly's feeder in the mimosa tree.

5

They drove to Tulsa in Dick Spearman's Ford Taurus, Dick and Marvelle in the front seat, because of their long legs, and Holly and Lawson in the back. The radio was on, playing Gussie Dell's "Neighbor Talk," and Holly could hear, over that, something shifting around in the trunk. "What is that?" she asked Dick.

"Boxes of hog sperm?" Marvelle said.

"Boxes of pamphlets from my company," Dick told Holly. "Hog sperm is shipped in dry ice," he informed Marvelle.

On the radio, Gussie Dell was telling a story about her grandson's Sunday-school drawing. "Jesus was wearing high heels," Gussie said. "No kidding. Nice blue pumps. I said,

'Norman, what a pretty picture,' because I have respect for Norman's creativity."

Outside, the streetlights had come on. Dick pulled onto the highway, south of Venus, and reminded them to put on their seat belts. Holly liked the way Dick drove. He went the speed limit, for one thing, and when cars passed him he didn't speed up, the way Burke always had. She looked out the window at the lights of farmhouses and listened to Gussie Dell, who was saying, "I think for myself. I don't swallow everything my church or anybody else tells me. I don't care if Norman puts Jesus in a garter belt."

"Can't you just see the switchboard at the radio station lighting up?" Lawson said.

Then "Neighbor Talk" was over, and they were closer to the state line. Dick talked about Sioux Falls, where he had grown up, and where his ex-wife still lived; he talked about Council Bluffs, where he lived now. Lawson talked about his own childhood in McAlester, Oklahoma.

"Did you know that Gene Rollison went to grade school in a one-room schoolhouse?" Holly asked Lawson. "He grew up in western Nebraska."

"I didn't know that," Marvelle said.

"He's embarrassed about it," Holly said. "I think it makes him feel unsophisticated compared to us."

"Gene Rollison is a state trooper," Lawson explained to Dick.

"I know," Dick said. "I saw in the paper that he got some kind of promotion."

"Really?" Holly asked.

"It's like in the army," Marvelle said. "You get a different title, but it's just another kind of bullshit."

"That's the cynical view of it, anyway," Dick said.

In the backseat Lawson smiled at Holly and moved closer to her. He was wearing a light-colored suit and a green tie with horses on it. "Are you as hungry as I am?" he asked her.

"That depends," Holly said. "How hungry are you?"

"Very. I forget to eat sometimes, living alone. It seems like too much trouble."

"It's lonely to cook for yourself," Dick said from the front seat. "I live on fast food."

"What is it with you men?" Marvelle said. "You're like children, or worse—the way you do things that will kill you."

"I'm not committing suicide," Dick said. "I'm just eating a hamburger."

There was silence in the car, during which Holly imagined she could see, even in the dark, Dick's neck reddening. "That was a bad choice of words," he told Marvelle.

They were in Tulsa soon after that, driving down a wide, tree-lined avenue. The restaurant was in a minimall southeast of downtown; when they got out of the car Holly could see the lights of skyscrapers in the distance.

Inside, a maitre d' in jeans and snakeskin boots showed them to their table. They ordered drinks, and Dick said he'd be happy to order dinner for all four of them. "If that's okay," he said. "I know what's good here."

"Pork ribs?" Marvelle asked him.

"Well, yes. Ribs and steaks," Dick said.

They were sitting at a table beneath a painting of two plump, seminude women relaxing on the grassy banks of a pond. Holly thought about how the painting was the opposite of the motorcycle poster still up in Marvelle's house, or the kinds of pictures she imagined Burke had up on his bedroom wall. For one thing, Holly thought, these women weren't holding in their stomachs.

"My ex-husband's girlfriend had her picture in a motorcycle magazine," she said, after finishing her first drink.

"Does she race motorcycles?" Dick asked.

"No," Holly said. "She rode on the back of one without her top on."

"I don't think I'd find that comfortable," Marvelle said.

She was ahead of everybody in terms of drinks. She'd almost finished her second whiskey sour, and Lawson had ordered another round. Holly wished he hadn't. Ever since Morgan's death, Marvelle was hard to be around once she started drinking. She got angry and belligerent. Holly watched her drink half of her third whiskey sour and slide down a little in her chair. "Can I ask you a question?" Marvelle said to Dick.

"I guess so," Dick said.

"Why don't you take better care of yourself? How come you don't like yourself better?"

"I do like myself," Dick told her. "It's my ex-wife I don't like."

"You think that," Marvelle said, "but you're like most men. You're self-centered, and you blame things on other people."

"What things?" Dick asked, but the waiter brought their salads then, and no one spoke until he retreated. Then Dick said, "I don't know which insult to respond to first."

Marvelle wasn't listening. She was on her feet, suddenly, motioning to the busy waiter. "You brought me the wrong salad dressing," she told him. "And why the hell didn't you bring me another drink?"

*A*fter they had eaten and their plates were cleared away— Marvelle and Dick not having exchanged another word— Lawson, who was sitting next to Holly, talked about each of the ten years of his bad marriage, and why he thought his wife would leave Rusty Fisher for someone less nice, with more money.

"I think you still love her," Holly said.

"You shouldn't hold on to the past," Dick told him, across the table. "It's always a mistake."

"What do you mean by *always*?" Marvelle asked. "I hate it when people think they can speak for everybody. And you're the one who doesn't like his ex-wife. Isn't that holding on to the past?"

"Listen," Dick said, "you and I got off to a bad start. I understand why, because I know what happened to you."

"You don't know anything about me." Marvelle got up, shoved back her chair, and walked straight out the front door.

"My ex-wife told me I wasn't good at making conversation," Dick told Lawson and Holly.

*O*ut in the dark parking lot, Marvelle got into the backseat of the car, next to Holly.

"Let's go somewhere and play pool," Lawson suggested.

"I'd just as soon go home," Marvelle told him.

"Come on," Lawson said. "Just a few games. Let's see if we can't have a little fun. Not that we haven't had fun so far."

"All right," Marvelle said, to Holly's surprise, and then she was quiet, looking out the window as they crossed the Arkansas River.

Holly saw the lights of the Sheraton Hotel, where she and Will Chaffe had spent the night once, Will having told his wife he was attending a workshop for restaurant owners. He and Holly had had dinner, swam in the indoor pool, and had room service deliver a bottle of champagne, which they drank in the bathtub. They'd started making love on the bathroom floor, then moved to the bed; Holly had awoken before daylight to a violent thunderstorm, and to Will on the telephone. "If it gets bad there, take the kids into the basement," she had heard him say.

He had hung up and stood naked in front of the window for a long time. Holly had watched him; she thought he might be crying. When he had finally turned around, she pretended to be asleep.

In the front seat now, Lawson was talking about marriage. He was telling Dick that his mother-in-law had never liked him. "Right from the start she thought I was a loser. I never knew why. How are you supposed to fight a thing like that?"

"I couldn't say," Dick said. Ever since Marvelle had gotten angry with him at the restaurant, he had refused to give a substantial answer to anything.

"Okay, I have my faults," Lawson said. "I'm aware of that. But I'd like to know just who my mother-in-law would have chosen for her daughter."

"It's always a mistake to live in the past," Marvelle said. "Just ask Dick."

"Don't I know it," Lawson said.

*D*ick pulled into the parking lot of a gray stucco building. "Mr. Buddy's Billiards," he said. "Should we give it a try, or keep on looking?"

"What difference does it make?" Marvelle asked, and so they parked and walked into the smokiest room Holly could remember, except for her old kitchen the time Burke, trying to make amends for some ugliness Holly couldn't any longer recall, accidentally set the bacon grease on fire.

Dick and Lawson found an open table under a poster in which a young blond woman in a bikini was holding a big wrench. The other tables were taken by men with tattoos, Holly noticed, and the kinds of girls Owen tried to date: big-haired young women wearing tight jeans and high-heeled boots. Holly liked the boots.

"I'll rack, if nobody minds," Dick said. "I know how to do it nice and tight."

"They don't allow that kind of talk in here," Lawson told him.

"Holly and I will play you two," Marvelle said. She chalked her pool cue, got two balls in on the break, and made three more before barely missing a combination bank shot.

"Don't worry about our pride," Lawson said. "Winning is the important thing."

"I think she knows that," Dick said.

Holly and Marvelle won the first three games, then Dick and Lawson won two, and Holly and Marvelle won the sixth. Two young, tattooed men at the next table—one of whom reminded Holly of a shorter, less attractive version of Gene Rollison—asked if the women wanted to play them for a round of beers. Before Holly or Marvelle had a chance to answer, Dick said, "We were just on our way out."

"What's your hurry?" Marvelle asked, as she, Holly, and Lawson followed him across the smoky room out to the cold parking lot. The spring nights were still cool.

"You don't want to play men who have tattoos up and down their arms," Dick said.

"Why not?" Marvelle said. "It takes courage to get a tattoo. It means you care about something, or somebody." She stopped in front of Dick's car. "I was married to a man with tattoos." She ignored the car door Dick opened for her and tried to get into the backseat with Holly, but Lawson had already gotten in, from the other side.

It was eleven-thirty as they left behind the lights of Tulsa for the dark highway back to Venus. Partway there, Lawson put his arm around Holly and said, "See that bright star?" He pointed out her window. "That's the North Star. That's how Dick is finding our way home."

"Luckily, I also have a road map," Dick said.

Lawson left his arm where it was, around Holly's shoulders. Holly liked Lawson but couldn't imagine feeling more for him than that, even if he weren't still in love with his wife. He was handsome; he was intelligent and lively and had a sense of humor, but she didn't feel her roots stirring, sitting here close to him. She didn't feel the way she had almost a year and a half earlier, when Will Chaffe, after jumping her car battery on a freezing January night in the Hearth's empty parking lot, suddenly kissed her. At that moment, despite every good reason not to, she kissed him back. She'd also suggested they go to her house. Owen had been spending the night with Burke.

"It's a pretty night," Lawson said to her.

"It is," Holly agreed.

Dick had the heat on in the car, which made her sleepy, and she rested her head back against Lawson's arm and closed her eyes. She listened to the "All-Night All-Time Hits" show on the radio and, vaguely, to Dick talking.

"I used to live in the country, too," he was saying to Marvelle. "But four or five years ago—after my wife divorced me, to be exact—I'd come home and there wouldn't be a soul to talk to. I moved into town, and now I have neighbors and such."

"I have my son, Curtis," Marvelle told him.

"What's going to happen when he moves away?" Dick asked. "When he goes away to college or finds a job?"

"Curtis is thirty-one," Marvelle said.

In the backseat, Holly could tell, even with her eyes closed, that Lawson's face was moving closer to hers. She could smell his aftershave. She opened her eyes a second before he kissed her. "Don't," she started to say, but right then a Roy Orbison song came on the radio, and she kissed Lawson back. She knew it was a mistake—she knew from experience, mainly with Burke, that certain songs sung by certain people could make her do almost anything, with anyone—but once she started kissing Lawson she didn't feel like stopping. He was breathing harder and pressing against her.

Suddenly Dick swerved to avoid hitting a deer, and Lawson, because he wasn't wearing his seat belt, was thrown against the door, away from Holly.

"I'm sorry about that," Dick said. "Are you okay?"

"I was a lot better a minute ago," Lawson told him.

"Put on your seat belt," Holly said. "You know how many deer there are this time of year."

Lawson did as he was told, then reached for her hand. "This is a big car," he announced. "There's about a half mile of space back here between me and Holly."

"It's roomy, isn't it?" Dick said. "That's why I bought it."

They were close to Venus now, driving past the billboard advertising Nyles Funeral Home, and past the VENUS, POPULATION 4,600 sign. They drove past the entrance to the Acres of Trailers Park, and Holly hoped that Owen was safe in bed, having an ordinary teenager's dream. A few minutes later Dick turned onto Old Highway 73 and pulled up in front of Holly's house, behind Marvelle's pickup.

"Don't bother getting out," Holly said quickly to Lawson and Dick as she and Marvelle got out of the car. "Thanks for everything."

"Especially the pool," Marvelle said. "That was more fun than I thought it would be."

"I'll bet," Dick said.

The women stood in the street and watched Dick's car lights disappear. "You weren't the best company," Holly said, "but you got better as the night went on."

"So did you," Marvelle said. She opened the door of her pickup, and Holly saw Morgan's old worn jacket on the seat, and a *Do It Yourself* home-repairs magazine. "Weren't you kissing Lawson?"

"Well, Roy Orbison was on the radio," Holly said.

She watched Marvelle drive away, noticing too late to warn her that her left taillight was out, and then she went inside and got ready for bed. She listened through her open bedroom window to the sounds of frogs in Spring Ditch. She missed, even more than she usually did, Owen being in the next room. She remembered her relief, the nights she fell asleep before he came in, waking up later and discovering he was home, in bed, his clothes in a heap on the floor.

Marvelle called just as Holly was thinking about calling her, to tell her about her taillight, and that Gene's one-room schoolhouse was once in an issue of *Life*. She'd just recalled that.

"Wendy's car is here," Marvelle said. "She and Curtis are in his bedroom with the door closed and the lights off."

"Maybe everything is okay, then."

"Maybe Roy Orbison is on the radio," Marvelle said.

After they hung up, Holly couldn't fall asleep. She was tired but restless, and she wished she had one of those heartbeat tapes people bought for babies, or a cassette of waterfall or ocean sounds. She was halfway into a dream before she realized that what she needed was a person there beside her.

6

*unch at the Hearth on Monday was slow. Marvelle left early to take a lunch special to Curtis at the Venus Feed 'n Seed, where he had a part-time job unloading hay bales; Will and Cleveland were in the kitchen, planning next week's specials. Holly, out in the dining room, had only two customers: Franklin Sanders and Beatrice Keel, at a booth, putting together the Venus United Methodist's newsletter. They were each having chicken with stewed tomatoes; Franklin was still eating his. Beatrice handed her unfinished plate to Holly.

"How do you spell *ecumenical?*" Franklin asked.

"It doesn't matter how you spell it," Beatrice told him. "It's still going to make people mad. You'll probably hear about it from my sister on 'Neighbor Talk.' "

"I'll take that chance," Franklin said.

"Will keeps a dictionary in his office," Holly told him. She went and got it for him, then poured him coffee as he looked up *tolerance* as well.

"Where has Marvelle Holman been keeping herself?" Beatrice asked Holly. "I worry about her."

"We hoped we'd see her here," Franklin said. "I brought her something." He took a cassette called *Grieving with God* out of his shirt pocket. "I know the look she's going to have on her face when you give her this, so just put it in her pickup. She'll know who it's from."

"God?" Beatrice asked.

"Very funny." Franklin handed the cassette to Holly. "And very far from it," he said to Beatrice.

Holly got herself a Coke and stood at the front counter, looking out the window at two children riding their bikes down the sidewalk in the shade of the elm trees—the elms that were still living, anyway. Behind Holly, Franklin and Beatrice were talking so quietly that she had to concentrate in order to eavesdrop.

"I've known your wife some forty-odd years," Beatrice said. "Don't forget that. I thought the two of you were a mistake from the start."

"God expects us to live with our mistakes," Franklin said.

"Bullshit," Beatrice told him.

"Then why do you live with yours?"

"Because I'm afraid," Beatrice said. "I'm entitled to be. I'm older than you are."

They asked Holly for more coffee; by the time she poured it they were arguing about whether, in the newsletter, birth announcements should come before weddings, and where to put obituaries.

"On a different page altogether," Beatrice said. "Don't clutter up the good news with the bad."

"Sometimes you completely miss the point of heaven," Franklin said.

"No, I don't," Beatrice told him. "I'm just not in a hurry to get there."

Franklin paid the check as Beatrice slowly got up from the booth. "You won't forget about the cassette, will you?" he said to Holly. "I'd give it to Marvelle myself, but I'm afraid she'd have me arrested for spiritual assault."

"I won't forget," she said.

She stood at the door as they left and watched Franklin help Beatrice into her old Ford Escort. Then Will came into the dining room, looking preoccupied and tired, and he and Holly moved three tables together in the back corner, next to the fireplace. A group called Teachers for a Friendlier Planet was coming in for dinner. They had caused some controversy in March by asking students to invent their own Friendly Planet slogans to print on T-shirts. Two juniors had come up with "Share Your Drugs" and a senior with "Have Sex with a Dweeb." Owen, to Holly's relief, thought the project too stupid to participate in.

"I think there will be ten teachers," Holly said. "Is that right?"

"I don't know," Will said. "I don't care." He reached across the table and put his hand on hers. "I don't know how to stop thinking about you," he said quietly. "It's making me crazy. I bet Morgan Holman loved somebody he couldn't have."

"Don't say that. That's not fair to anyone."

"You underestimate love," Will said. "I don't think you know what it is."

Holly took her hand away and went into the kitchen for the largest tablecloth they had, which turned out to be still drying in the small laundry room off the kitchen. She went out the back door and sat on the hood of her Chevette. She'd parked it under the spreading branches of the oak tree next door, behind Magro's Shoes; the branches reached over the wire fence. She could smell the honeysuckle from the tangle of bushes and spindly trees that grew back there. She thought about how, at this time last year, she and Will would have stood in the dim, narrow space between the Hearth and the shoe store, with their hands on each other; two years before that, when she and Burke were getting a divorce, Will would have been telling her that it was better to be alone than it was to be lonely and married.

Will came out the back door now, bringing Holly coffee and a piece of peach pie. "I didn't mean what I said," he told her. "I'm not going to kill myself over you. That would be stupid. I wouldn't get to see you anymore."

"You wouldn't get to see me bending over the ice cream freezer," Holly told him.

"That's a good example of what I mean," Will said. "You don't know shit about love."

"Okay, I'm sorry," Holly said.

"What kind of person do you think I am?"

"A good person," Holly told him. "Really."

Will leaned against her car, and he and Holly shared the slice of pie, donating the crust to a bird or a squirrel—whoever got to it first, Will said, whatever creature was having a happier, luckier day than he was.

They walked back into the kitchen together. "Evelyn called," Cleveland told Will. "She sounded upset about something."

"For a change," Will said, and went off to use the phone in the dining room.

$\mathcal{H}$olly was scheduled to come back to the restaurant late in the afternoon to work the dinner shift; in between she went to the Venus Nursery and bought impatiens and pansies. At home she planted them in the space she had left in her garden. As she worked, hot and sweaty under the cloudy sky, she sometimes felt that Lawson was watching her from next door. He came outside once to carry in a Labrador for a teenage girl—the dog had come to a complete stop at the foot of the stairs—and he waved to Holly.

At four-thirty she showered, changed into her uniform, and drove back to the Hearth. Will wasn't there yet. Holly sat in the kitchen with Sue-Ellis Howard and Cleveland and ate fried chicken. Sue-Ellis was related to Will; she was his wife's cousin. She was just two years younger than Holly, though she and Holly hadn't gone to school together. Sue-Ellis had grown up in Ferrisville. She had a daughter who was a year older than Owen.

"Listen to my morning," she told Holly and Cleveland as the three of them were eating at the scuffed wooden table. "My first ex-husband called me at seven, to say that he was broke and that the police were after him for leaving a Gas 'N' Grocery without paying. I was supposed to lend him five hundred dollars. Then, a little later, my second ex-husband's girlfriend called to say that he—Randall—had just hit her. I was supposed to solve that problem, too."

"What did you do?" Cleveland asked.

"I went back to sleep after the first phone call," Sue-Ellis said. "After the second one, I got up and took a shower."

"You people with your ex's," Cleveland said. "I married one person and stayed married."

"So far," Sue-Ellis told him.

She stood up and carried her plate over to the big dishwasher; then she got herself a bowl of ice cream and sat back down. A few customers, Holly knew, had complained to Will about Sue-Ellis's tight uniform. According to Will, they felt it reminded people—people who knew, anyway—that she had once worked as a dancer at the Truck City Bar, in Topeka. Sue-Ellis was twenty pounds or so overweight, and Holly admired her for not trying to hide it and not caring who knew.

The teachers came in at six-thirty. She knew several of them: a second-grade teacher she'd had herself; a man who taught at Owen's high school; and Crystal Turner, the sixth-grade teacher Holly had recently seen talking to Owen outside the video store. Holly listened to pieces of their conversation as she gave them their drinks, salads, and dinners. They talked about starting an international pen-pal program.

"Let's not take any chances," one of the middle-school teachers said. "No drug-producing countries, and no students exchanging letters with members of the opposite sex."

"Why risk letters at all? Let's just send Hallmark cards to the ambassadors," the high school teacher said. "Let's send flowers and balloons to the heads of American companies."

"I don't see how sarcasm is going to help us make a decision," Crystal Turner said.

"I never said it would help," he told her.

Holly cleared the table and brought their desserts; then she sat in the overly warm kitchen and made out their separate checks.

"Walking past that table gives me the creeps," Sue-Ellis said. She was standing at the counter behind Holly, putting French dressing on two salads. "They have that look. I can't describe it. I had to pee a minute ago, and I almost raised my hand to ask permission."

"Did you finish high school?" Holly asked her.

"Not exactly," Sue-Ellis said.

"My son wants to quit. That's why it's on my mind."

"Oh, well. Boys," Sue-Ellis said. "The only way you're going to make them like school is if you let them sleep with their teachers."

She took the salads into the dining room, and Holly followed her, bringing the teachers their checks. Most of them were getting ready to leave, the women picking up their purses, and Holly said hello to Crystal Turner.

"I thought that was you," Crystal said. "How are you? How is Owen? I haven't seen him in a long time."

"He's fine. He's living with his father for the time being," Holly said.

Crystal picked up her check and walked toward the register, and Holly guessed that the day she'd seen Crystal talking to Owen outside Adventure Video Crystal hadn't really remembered who Owen was. She'd just remembered having him one year as a student. For a moment Holly was tempted to go after Crystal and tell her. Crystal Turner had been Owen's favorite teacher—the only teacher he'd ever liked— and it bothered Holly that Owen wasn't special to her. But Crystal seemed to be in a hurry; she had already paid and was walking out the door, and Holly stayed where she was, clearing away the dessert plates and the coffee cups and removing the tablecloth. Will helped her separate the tables and move them back where they belonged.

At nine o'clock Holly left the restaurant with Sue-Ellis, who had asked for a ride home. They walked out of the kitchen into the warm night. As they got in the car Sue-Ellis said, "My daughter dropped me off and promised she'd be back by now. Why do kids lie so much? How come they don't figure out it's easier to tell the truth?"

"It's not always easier," Holly said.

"It is for me. I tell the truth, and people stay out of my way."

"Is that what you want?" Holly asked. "I mean, don't you get lonely?"

Sue-Ellis fastened her seat belt and accidentally pushed one of the tape-player controls, ejecting Holly's Roy Orbison cassette. "Well, I have a cat," she said.

Holly drove down Venus Avenue past the park, where the streetlights illuminated the leafy trees; she turned left on Restwell Drive and pulled up in front of Sue-Ellis's duplex. It was next to the cemetery where Morgan was buried, as well as Holly's father. Holly had thought about renting the left side of the duplex after her divorce from Burke, before her mother had lent her the down payment for a house. "Are you sure?" Marvelle had said. "Can't you find someplace more depressing?" But on the plus side, as Owen had pointed out, they wouldn't have noisy neighbors.

"This must be a quiet place to live," Holly said as Sue-Ellis was getting out of the car.

"It is," Sue-Ellis said. "It's really dead around here."

Holly was still smiling as she pulled away from the curb and continued down Restwell Drive. Then she saw Marvelle sitting outside the cemetery entrance in her pickup. Holly parked behind her and walked up to her open window.

"What are you doing here?" she asked. "You won't be able to find Morgan's grave at night."

"I had to get out of the house," Marvelle said. "Wendy Dell was over, baking cookies, and she kept talking about the vice principal at her school. 'You wouldn't believe the size of his desk,' she kept saying. That's who she was with at the mall, Holly. I'd bet money on it."

"Unlock your other door."

Holly got into the pickup on the passenger side. "I gave Sue-Ellis a ride home," she told Marvelle. "That's how I happened to see you."

"Did she let out her uniform yet?" Marvelle asked.

"No," Holly said. "I don't think Will asked her to."

Marvelle was resting her hands on the steering wheel; Holly could see her wedding ring glinting in the darkness. Outside, the crickets and cicadas were making a racket—not so much in the cemetery, it seemed to Holly, as in the empty field behind it, which would eventually become part of the cemetery, too, she imagined. The night after Holly's father died, Holly's mother had dreamed that he was in a beautiful place with interesting people. "Sounds like Restwell Cemetery to me," Holly had told her.

"Honey, that's a terrible thing to say," her mother had said. "I worry about the way your mind works. Why don't you ever look on the bright side of things?"

"Sometimes there is no bright side," Holly had told her.

Holly remembered that conversation as she looked from Marvelle's wedding ring to the dark field outside. See, she said privately to her mother, what bright, happy thing would occur to you right now?

"Was the Hearth busy tonight?" Marvelle asked her.

"Not really," Holly said. "There was a going-out-of-business sale at Venus Bargain Center."

"That's where Morgan used to buy his boots."

Marvelle took her keys out of the ignition. "Let's walk around a little," she said to Holly. They got out of the pickup and climbed the steep bank of grass into the graveyard. The night had become windy. Streaks of clouds were blowing past the moon, and in the distance—from Sue-Ellis's porch, probably—was the sound of a wind chime.

"Morgan's grave is somewhere to the right," Marvelle said, "on the border between the Hope and Tranquility sections. He's not really located in either one."

They walked past the weeping angel, a big stone carving with outstretched wings hovering over the monument of Ida Louise Knowles, Venus's ex-mayor. Holly was familiar with this section; she'd visited the cemetery once a week after her father died, for almost a year. That was when she wanted to

divorce Burke but couldn't yet, somehow. In those days the
cemetery had made her feel better. She remembered thinking: These people can't get up and drop firecrackers into gopher holes; and, on really bad days: Nobody here is going to
lose control over his temper.

"I wonder what Morgan would think, knowing I was
wandering around here in the dark," Marvelle said.

"Nothing," Holly told her. "Isn't that the point? If I were
going to kill myself, it would be so that I wouldn't have to
think at all anymore."

Marvelle was in front of the Life Everlasting section. "How
comforting," she told Holly. "So now I'm supposed to worry
about you shooting yourself?"

"That's not what I meant. Sometimes I don't say things the
way I mean them."

"I think you say just what you mean," Marvelle told her. She
walked a few feet away from Holly, up the small hill into the
older part of the cemetery where the gravestones were smaller
and not quite straight. "I wish Morgan were buried here," she
said. "Then it would have happened a long time ago, and I
could think about suicide romantically, the way that you do."

"I don't," Holly told her.

She had followed Marvelle into the older section and was
standing in front of the gravestone of a baby.

" 'The angels will know her name,' " Holly read aloud, in
the moonlight. "Isn't that pretty?" she asked Marvelle.

"Very cheerful," Marvelle said.

Holly followed her down the hill through the section
where Morgan's grave was, somewhere among all the
others—as new as it was it was no longer the most recent.

"It's not that I don't feel bad for Morgan," Holly told Marvelle. "It's not like I don't wish it had never happened."

"I think you just wish it had happened to you."

Holly stopped walking. She was standing at the foot of a new grave—the dirt freshly turned, no proper gravestone, and the branches of an oak tree behind it moving eerily in the wind. "You think I want to be dead?" she asked Marvelle.

"Not dead, exactly," Marvelle said. "More like slowly dying, so that you don't miss anything, but you get to feel bad the whole time."

"That is so mean," Holly said tearfully.

"Don't do that," Marvelle told her. "Don't get moody every time I tell the truth about something." She took Holly's arm and led her down to the quiet street. "It's strange here at night, isn't it? Like a drive-in after the movie's over and everybody's gone home."

"I think it's peaceful," Holly said defensively.

Marvelle said good night, drove off in her pickup, and left Holly standing alone in the empty street. The clouds had moved off, making more stars visible; all at once the cemetery looked too real and final to Holly. She got into her car and headed home.

She had just turned off Venus Avenue onto Hyacinth when she saw Owen standing in front of the Hyacinth Apartments with Crystal Turner. They looked like they were about to kiss, or had just kissed; in any case, Holly thought, they seemed to be thinking about kissing, and without meaning to, she speeded up, forgetting the stop sign at the corner.

7

he car she hit was Reese Nyles's—not the black Cadillac
he used at the funeral home, but the ancient brown Pon-
tiac he had bought almost two decades ago from Burke, when
Holly and Burke were just out of high school. Reese, just
back from Vietnam, had been serious and watchful, checking
things out from behind his thick glasses.

"This was my fault," Holly said, after she and Reese got
out of their cars. Then she noticed Reese's bare feet and his
unbuttoned shirt. "What's the matter with you?"

"Jenny Dyer," he said. "She left Rusty Fisher and came to
my house for a drink, and then she left my house and I can't
figure out where she went." His car door was open, and
Holly could see three empty beer cans on the floor.

He and Holly stood in the middle of the intersection and inspected their cars. His, Holly thought, looked okay, at least in the moonlight; it was so full of dents and rust you couldn't tell, anyway. But hers was damaged. She got back in it, to move it out of the intersection, and discovered that it wouldn't start.

"Give it more gas," Reese shouted.

"Keep quiet," Holly said. "Don't wake anybody up." She got out of her car and told Reese to get back into his. "And stay there," she told him. "I mean it. Don't move."

She walked up Hyacinth one block, to the public library, and called Gene Rollison from the pay phone out front. "This is Holly Parker," she said when he answered. "I know this is asking another big favor, but I didn't know who else to call."

"Has your son been cutting up the newspaper again?" Gene asked.

"No," Holly told him. "This was my mistake. I smashed into Reese Nyles's car, and he's had a few beers, and I don't want him to get into trouble because of me. Also, I can hardly afford my car insurance as it is."

"I don't know that you'll be able to afford my fee," Gene said, "but I'll be there in twenty minutes."

Holly walked back to find Reese sitting on the pavement with his head in his hands. He and Holly pushed her Chevette out of the intersection and against the curb, and they parked Reese's car behind it, under a streetlight, and sat in the front seat, waiting for Gene.

"I renovated my bathroom for Jenny," Reese said after a few minutes. "I bought her a canopy bed."

"Sometimes things just don't work out," Holly told him.

"Why don't you women tell us that before we spend so much money?" Then he put his hand apologetically on Holly's shoulder. "Never mind. It's not your fault."

Holly could see his face in the glow from the streetlight—how tired his eyes looked when he took off his glasses. He'd gotten married, after he came back from Vietnam, to a girl who'd been a friend of Holly's in high school. She'd divorced him a year later for somebody her own age. "Reese wasn't enough fun," she had told Holly.

He had his eyes closed now, his head back against the seat. Holly watched for Gene's headlights. She thought about Crystal Turner, who was thirty or so, and not even Owen's type. Crystal didn't wear makeup or mousse up her hair, and she jogged every day after school—Holly often saw her running past the Hearth. Holly couldn't imagine what drew her and Owen together. Owen's idea of exercise was climbing on his dirt bike or pressing down on the accelerator of his father's truck. But then Holly remembered that when Owen was Crystal's student, he'd come home talking about ecosystems and rain forests and Ms. Turner's solar-system mobile, and for a while, until Burke bribed him with a fast-food hamburger, he wouldn't eat meat.

Reese opened his eyes. He buttoned and tucked in his shirt. "What is it that women want?" he asked Holly.

"Somebody who looks up to them," Holly said.

*G*ene Rollison drove up then—in his Saturn, rather than his state-police car, and Holly explained to him about not seeing the stop sign.

"Don't take all the blame," Reese said. "I was drinking and driving."

"Reese has been out looking for Jenny Dyer," Holly told Gene, "and in my opinion he's not drunk so much as upset."

"I didn't say I was drunk," Reese said.

"I'll drive him home, and you follow us in his car," Gene told Holly. "Then I'll call the wrecker at the Conoco station to come and get your Chevette."

Reese handed Holly the keys, and she got in the driver's seat and started his car. It was as awkward and boatlike as Holly remembered. The seat was torn, and in spite of the almost twenty years since Burke had been in it, she thought the car still smelled like him. She had a sudden, embarrassing memory of her panties once lying on the floor of the backseat.

Holly hadn't known where, exactly, Reese lived, which turned out to be down the road from the small, new housing development in which Will Chaffe lived, on the eastern edge of Venus. She had driven out in this direction more than once, when Will's wife and children were out of town. She followed Gene a mile or so further down the road, and then off to the left, into Reese's driveway. He had a narrow prefabricated house set back under oak trees, and all the lights were on. Holly walked into the house behind Gene and Reese—Gene taller than Reese, more solid, and more polite; he held the door open for Holly. When he closed it behind her Holly heard John Wayne say, on the TV Reese had left on, "Don't you know you can never trust a woman?"

"I do now," Reese said.

They all stood in the living room, with its gray carpeting and glossy furniture. "Well," Gene said. "How about some coffee, Reese?"

"No, thanks," Reese said. "I want to show you something."

He led Gene and Holly down the hallway to the renovated bathroom, which had a two-person bathtub with a Jacuzzi, and then he showed them the bedroom with the white canopy bed. He lay down on it.

"Jenny's not going to find another bed she likes this much," he told them.

"It's very attractive," Holly said.

"At least you've made some home improvements," Gene said.

Holly looked at the white comforter Reese had his dirty feet on, and at the picture of Jenny that was on his bureau. It was one of those fashion/model shots you could get done now in malls. Jenny was wearing a cowboy hat and a black leotard, which reminded Holly of her only Jenny Dyer encounter, in an aerobics class at the Y a few years earlier. Jenny, right up in front, wearing a lycra outfit, had said, "Couldn't we have the class go for an hour and a half instead of just an hour?"

"Stay put tonight," Gene told Reese. "I don't want to see you back in your car again."

"Of course not," Reese said. "I hear you." He closed his eyes and was breathing regularly before Holly and Gene even left the room. They went into the kitchen, where Gene used the phone to call the wrecker; they turned off the television and lights and walked out under the trees.

"He has a nice, private place here," Gene said, walking slowly next to Holly in the darkness. They were close enough to touch, and for a moment Gene brushed against her, his arm against her shoulder, his hand against her leg. Holly moved closer to him just as he said, "Excuse me," and she backed away a step, feeling foolish. Then they were at his car, Gene unlocking Holly's door.

*A*s they drove back through Venus, Gene said, "When I mentioned coffee I meant that I wanted him to make us some."

"I'll make you coffee at my house," Holly said. "All Reese could think about was Jenny. Here he thought she'd come back—you know how it is. You feel like you're never going to get over it."

"I know," Gene said.

"I guess you do."

"Well, I wasn't thinking especially about Marvelle. I was thinking about high school, when I was always heartbroken about one girl or another."

"That's hard to believe."

"You didn't know me then," Gene told her.

Holly watched him put on his turn signal before he down-shifted, and then shift again and speed up. "Did you ever have a crush on somebody older, when you were a teenager?" she asked him.

"I liked a senior cheerleader. I must have been fifteen or so."

"I mean somebody much older," Holly said as he turned off Venus Avenue. "I saw my son, Owen, tonight with his thirty-year-old sixth-grade teacher."

"What do you mean, with?" Gene asked.

"Almost kissing."

"Wow," Gene said. "I would have given a lot to kiss my sixth-grade teacher." He parked in front of Holly's house. "I mean, that's how twelve-year-old boys can be."

"I'm sure," Holly said.

In the kitchen, while the coffee brewed, they sat across from each other at the table. Holly felt so self-conscious about her dirty uniform that she went into her bedroom and came back with a sweater over it.

"I bet your son's good-looking," Gene said then.

"Thank you," Holly said right away, before realizing he might not be referring to her part in Owen's good looks.

"You're welcome," Gene told her, "but what I meant was: What else would a thirty-year-old woman see in someone so young?"

"Oh," Holly said, feeling embarrassed and foolish for the second time that night, and angry at Gene for making her feel that way. She looked down at the table and then at her reflection in the window. "I see what you mean. You mean the way that men always want women who are younger than they are, because all they care about is how women look."

"Some men," Gene said. "And I'd take out the 'always.' "

"Well, I think you should meet Owen before you decide he's handsome but stupid."

"I never said he was stupid," Gene told her. "How come you're so quick to take offense at everything I say?"

"How should I know?" Holly said.

The coffee was done, and she got up and took as long as she could to pour it. By this time, even though she could see herself overreacting, everything about him irritated her. For example, when she heard him move his chair a little, behind her, she imagined that he was lining it up just right for safety's sake, so that it wouldn't accidentally tip back or trip some unsuspecting person like her son, who'd inherited her stupidity and nothing else. And now, when she turned around and he looked at her, she felt that he was looking at her with that well-meaning, wholesome expression his family had been handing down for generations.

"What is it?" Holly said sharply.

"I was just thinking about your accident, about whether you felt okay," Gene said.

"I probably feel better than I look," Holly told him.

"No," Gene said. "I don't think that's ever true."

Holly handed him his coffee and sat down with her own, trying to figure out what that meant, exactly, and if it might possibly be a compliment.

"All right," she said after a minute. "Thank you."

"You're welcome," Gene said.

They drank their coffee. Holly was tired, finally. She listened to the wind, which had picked up outside. She could hear it in the trees, rustling the leaves; she could hear a branch of the pecan tree in her backyard knocking against the house.

"Can you feel your trailer shake when it's windy like this?" she asked Gene, to be friendlier.

"Yes," he said. "It rocks a little. You'll have to come over one windy night."

He stood up and put his cup on the counter. He had on a green shirt she'd seen him wear once before, at the Hearth; now that he wasn't criticizing her or her son, she could see how good that shirt looked on him—the way it fit across his chest, and how the color was a shade darker than his eyes.

Holly walked him outside. On her dark porch, Gene looked at the open fields to the south. "You call me if you're ever nervous here alone," he said suddenly. "I don't care how late it is."

His voice was gentle, and what he said reminded her that she was alone. He even sounded as if he worried about her. She turned toward the veterinary clinic next door, so that Gene couldn't see her face, and said, "I'm okay. Now that Lawson Dyer's separated, he often stays late next door."

Gene looked at her as if she'd offended him. "I'll see you," he said, and walked across her yard to his car. The moon was bright enough for her to see him not wave as he drove off.

*I*nside, even though it was after eleven, Holly called Burke from her bedroom phone and told him about Owen and Crystal Turner.

"Jesus Christ," Burke said. "She's almost as old as you are, Holly." In the background, Holly heard Annette singing along to a country-and-western song.

"We should do something about it," Holly said. "We should talk to him, at least."

"Owen," she heard Burke shouting, "your mother wants to talk to you."

"I didn't mean now, and I didn't mean just me," Holly said, but Burke wasn't on the phone any longer.

"What, Mom?" Owen said a moment later.

Holly sat down on her bed. "Honey, what happened to that girl you were dating?"

"Who?" Owen said. "Why are you asking?"

"I saw you tonight with Crystal Turner."

Owen didn't say anything. Holly could hear Annette's voice so clearly she could make out the words. "So what?" Owen said finally.

"She's too old for you. And it's not a good idea for her, either. She could get into a lot of trouble."

"What do you mean?" Owen said.

"Use your head, honey. What do you think the parents of her sixth-graders would say, seeing her with a sixteen-year-old?"

Owen was quiet again. Holly could hear Burke say, "Wynonna doesn't need your help, Annette."

Then Owen said to Holly, "Crystal doesn't care what people think. She says that most people don't think. She says that everybody's free to do what they want but that most people don't know what they want."

"But I suppose she does," Holly said.

"She says a lot of other things, too," Owen told her, in the enthusiastic voice Holly hadn't heard him use much since the sixth grade. "Like yesterday, she was telling me about this ginger thing she was doing in school."

"Ginger?" Holly asked.

"This male/female thing," Owen said. "About how we're different from each other but exactly the same except that girls have feelings that guys aren't smart enough to understand." He paused a moment. "Guys are still cool, though," he said. "It's not their fault their fathers screwed them up."

*H*olly changed into her nightgown. She had had a headache ever since she hit Reese's car, and it had gotten worse during her talk with Owen. She went into the kitchen for aspirin and a glass of water; she looked at Gene's cup on the counter and thought about what she should have said on the porch, earlier, when Gene told her she could call him: "I promise I will," or "Thank you," or "You can call me, too, for any reason." Instead, she'd mentioned another man's name.

She rinsed out Gene's cup and went back to the bedroom, stopping for a moment in the hallway to look at a picture of Owen, taken almost twelve years ago, when he was five, when her biggest worry about him was whether Burke would take the training wheels off his bicycle too soon.

In bed, in order to fall asleep, she imagined Gene Rollison in his bed. Did he sleep naked, she wondered. Did he ever wonder if she did? Would they ever have the chance to find out? And asleep, finally, she dreamed that her father was calling her long distance, saying, "I'm not dead, honey. I'm not even sick. I've just moved to Nebraska."

8

olly's car was fixed by Saturday. Marvelle came over at eight to give her a ride to the auto-body shop. Afterward, Holly was going to follow Marvelle out to the cemetery, to help her plant flowers on Morgan's grave. In the back of Marvelle's truck were flats of impatiens and marigolds. "I want to cover the whole grave with flowers," Marvelle said. She had her Feed 'n Seed visor on the seat next to her, on top of the unopened *Grieving with God* cassette from Franklin Sanders.

"Let's listen to this God tape," Holly said, picking it up. "I'll unwrap it." When Marvelle didn't answer, Holly said, "You used to go to church, so it must mean something to you."

"I used to sit there and wonder what other people prayed for," Marvelle said. "I stopped praying a long time ago."

"And now you just don't go."

"You're hardly one to talk," Marvelle told Holly. "What do you believe in? Anyway, I don't have to go to church. Church comes to me." She took the tape from Holly and put it back on the seat.

"Franklin Sanders comes to you," Holly said. "That's not the same thing."

"Isn't it?" Marvelle asked. "Do you think Franklin ever goes anywhere without God?"

*A*t the cemetery later, Marvelle was quiet as she and Holly unloaded the pickup and carried the flats over to Morgan's grave. It was a hot morning. Holly could see a crop duster flying low over a distant field. There was a burial going on in the Forgiveness section; Holly heard a sentence from the Lord's Prayer, and then an amen. After the mourners drove away, Reese Nyles walked over in his black suit and helped Holly turn on the rusty water spigot outside the caretaker's shed.

"I see your car's back in shape," he said, pointing to Holly's Chevette. "I wish I could say the same thing for my love life."

"You haven't heard from Jenny?"

"No, but I think my answering machine might not be working. And maybe she feels funny about calling me at work." He took off his jacket, lay it over a gravestone, and helped Holly carry Marvelle's big watering can over to Morgan's grave. "I like this kind of work," he said to Holly and to Marvelle, who was planting impatiens. "I should have been a gardener."

"Well, you are, in a way," Marvelle said.

"I think of myself as a facilitator," Reese told her, "kind of a mediator between the living and the dead. Sometimes I feel like I have a foot in each place."

"I know just what you mean," Marvelle said.

"No, you don't," Reese told her. "The only person who maybe knew was Morgan." He watered the impatiens for her, picked up his jacket, and walked off toward his big, black car.

"That wasn't about you; he's just going through a bad time because of Jenny Dyer," Holly told Marvelle, although a moment later, looking at the rows of graves, she thought he might have been right to say what he had. What did Marvelle know about death compared to people who'd seen it up close? What did she, herself, know?

She knelt down to plant marigolds. She and Marvelle had the cemetery to themselves now. The only sounds were chickadees chattering in a mulberry tree behind them. It was midafternoon by the time they finished planting, and they walked up the hill to see how Morgan's grave looked from there. The flowers were beautiful, but they made the grave gaudy, Holly thought, like a too bright boat on a green sea.

*T*hat afternoon Holly and Marvelle went for a walk out at Marvelle's house, following a path through the open field across from the garage.

"I read that if we do above-the-waist arm movements as we walk, it's as good for us as aerobics," Holly said.

"I want to go for an ordinary walk, with my arms doing ordinary things," Marvelle told her.

They followed the trail up a wooded hill, across a ditch, and along a grassy ridge from which they could see all the way to Black Creek. Then they turned around and walked back. Morgan had maintained the trail by driving it once a week; now it was overgrown with weeds. "I'll have to drive the jeep up here myself now," Marvelle said as she and Holly were coming back across the field in the late-afternoon light. "Curtis never does."

"Why don't you tell him to?"

"I don't like to," Marvelle said. "I don't like to make him do things he doesn't want to do."

They walked carefully through the wild rosebushes at the edge of the field. Then they were back at Marvelle's house. Inside, Curtis was lying on the couch, watching television.

"I'm about to make margaritas," Marvelle told him. "Do you want one?"

"Shit, yes," he said.

Holly and Marvelle drank theirs in the kitchen while Holly leafed through *Fate: True Reports of the Strange and Unknown*— a magazine Curtis subscribed to. Marvelle stood at the window, looking out at the woods. She had a second drink before Holly was halfway through her first one. Then, ten minutes later, Marvelle poured herself a third. Holly was watching her.

"Don't say it," Marvelle said.

"I didn't say a word."

They were going to the truck stop that night for dinner. Marvelle poured the rest of her drink into a paper cup and carried it with her.

"This is your last chance to come with us," she said to Curtis as she and Holly walked through the dim living room on their way out. "Otherwise you'll have to eat leftovers." Curtis, engrossed in a police-show rerun, didn't answer.

Holly drove. The gravel road was shaded now. "Neighbor Talk" was on the radio, and Gussie Dell was giving out her recipe for strawberry pie. "I do this every year," she said, "and not once have any of my friends served it to me. Why do they think I announce it? People always expect unselfish behavior from others. Well, forget it. Everybody else is just as selfish as you are." Then she said, "I take that back. My grandson, Norman, did an unselfish thing. He donated his Hershey bar to the fish in the aquarium at his pediatrician's office. It killed every last one." Gussie Dell sang a song, then: "Yellow Submarine." "What do those words mean?" she asked her listeners. "What were the Beatles trying to tell us?"

*H*olly exited the highway at the truck stop and parked; she followed the uneven path Marvelle took into the restaurant. They sat in a window booth, and the waitress, Leona, brought them menus. "The meatloaf is good," she told them. "The chicken looks dried out. The soup seems okay."

"I'll have the dried-out soup," Marvelle said.

"We'll just take a look at the menus," Holly told Leona. "Meanwhile, we'll both have coffee."

"Is that Burke and Owen and Annette back there, or am I seeing things?" Marvelle asked.

"Probably both," Holly said. She turned around and saw Burke and Annette standing up in the smoking section, getting ready to leave, still puffing away. Owen wasn't smoking. He was poking at something on his plate. He got up then. He and Annette stopped at Holly and Marvelle's booth on their way out. Burke ignored them and went to pay the check.

"What didn't you eat?" Holly asked Owen.

"Chicken-fried steak," he said. "Crystal says they cook it in lard."

"That's why it's so good," Annette offered. She flipped back her long hair. "We come here every Saturday," she said to Holly. "It's our night out."

"How sad!" Marvelle exclaimed. "My God, Holly, is that what your life was like?"

Leona came through, right then, shouldering a big tray of food, and Holly wasn't sure how much Annette and Owen had heard. But Owen was almost smiling, and he waved to Holly from the parking lot just before he got into Burke's van.

"I hope I wasn't rude," Marvelle told Holly, "but somebody needs to be truthful with her."

Holly was distracted by Lawson Dyer and Dick Spearman, who were standing outside the window in a pansy border, knocking on the glass.

"Come on in!" Marvelle said loudly. "We're just about to make pigs of ourselves!"

A minute later Lawson and Dick were sitting down at the booth with Holly and Marvelle, Lawson asking Holly if it was all right after he was already sitting next to her.

"This is a coincidence," Marvelle said to Dick. "I had a dream about you last night. You and I were in a rowboat with

Franklin Sanders. He's the minister of the Methodist church."

"Nobody ever dreams about me," Lawson said. "Even my wife didn't, so far as I know."

"She moved out of Rusty Fisher's house," Holly told him.

"Well, I'm sorry for him," Lawson said. "I really am. I know how that feels."

"Get over it," Marvelle told Lawson. "Nobody wants to hear about it anymore."

Leona came over and took their orders; then the restaurant emptied out a little. It was almost dark outside. The radio was on, and after Leona brought their salads they could hear the end of Gussie Dell's program, where she sent out congratulations and condolences to people.

"'This one is for my sister, Beatrice,' Gussie said, "who's back in the hospital for tests. Honey, I'll be there in the morning, right after church. Save me a piece of toast." Then she said, as always, "This is your neighbor talking. I talk all the time, but only once a week on your radio."

Leona brought their dinners—macaroni and cheese for Holly and Marvelle, meat loaf and french fries for Dick, spaghetti for Lawson. They were halfway through eating when there was a commotion at a booth in the Truck Drivers Only section. A man in a cowboy hat, who was talking on the phone, loudly said, "I don't care if Oprah thinks I'm a pig!" He slammed down the receiver and threw his water glass at the pie case, which shattered.

"There goes dessert," someone said, and Holly heard a few people laugh.

"What's funny about that?" Marvelle said.

"Not a thing," Dick told her. "People laugh because it makes them uncomfortable, that's all."

"What do you suppose his wife is upset about?" Lawson asked.

𝒟inner was over, it seemed to Holly. No one felt like eating after that. They paid their checks and spent a few minutes in Boot City. Dick and Lawson looked at belt buckles, and Holly and Marvelle looked at lizards preserved inside paperweights.

Outside the wind was blowing around dust and bits of trash. The four of them stood next to Dick's Ford Taurus and watched bats circle the big, lit-up sign over the truck stop. "They're sweet animals," Lawson said. "Shy as children."

"Did you hear there's going to be a meteor shower tonight?" Dick asked Holly and Marvelle. "It was on the radio. Let's go someplace where we can see it."

They decided to drive in Dick's car out to Pinnacle Mountain—a scenic lookout Holly hadn't been up to since high school. It was twenty miles southwest of Venus, less than that from the truck stop, and not on a mountain or even that high a hill, as Holly remembered, just a hill that was higher than anything else around it.

On their way there, in the backseat, Holly kept her distance from Lawson, then moved a little closer to him when he said, "You look pretty tonight." He put his hand on her leg as she listened to Dick talk about his mother, who, at the age of seventy-four, hoped to fall in love and remarry. Dick's father had been dead for six years.

"She goes to dances at the senior citizens center," Dick said. "Once in a while she'll have a widower in for dinner. Do you know what they talk about?"

"Birth control?" Lawson asked.

"Shut up," Marvelle told him. "The people they used to be married to, I bet," she said to Dick.

"That's right. That's how they get to know each other."

The rest of the drive was quiet. Marvelle fell asleep, and Holly closed her eyes and pretended to be. At one point she heard Dick and Lawson talk softly about the shortened life expectancy of dairy cows kept isolated from one another. Holly was almost asleep herself when they arrived at Pinnacle Mountain, and they had to wake Marvelle, who got out of the car and walked over to the lookout and almost off it.

"Hold on," Dick said, taking her arm and pulling her back, though it wasn't that steep a drop-off, Holly knew; once, when she was fifteen and wouldn't let Burke reach all the way up under her skirt, he'd jumped off the lookout and landed just four or five feet down, on a sticker bush.

They sat on a blanket Dick had in his trunk and looked out at the widely spaced lights of farmhouses. "I bet half the population of Venus was started up here," Marvelle said. "This is where everybody used to come in high school."

"So to speak," Lawson said.

"People who haven't had sex in a long time talk about it a lot," Marvelle told him.

"I don't blame them," Lawson said.

The moon was up and the sky was full of stars, but as far as Holly could tell none of them were falling. "When is the meteor shower supposed to start?" she asked.

"That's what I can't remember," Dick said. "I'm thinking ten or eleven."

Holly lay back on the blanket, next to Lawson, and watched the sky. She could make out the Milky Way and the Big Dipper, but that was all. She didn't know much about astronomy, or any kind of science. She hadn't been a good student, and Burke had sat behind her in her sophomore science class, whispering, "Your hair smells like perfume," or "I can't look at your neck without wanting to lick it," and other romantic things she would replay to herself in bed at night. The distance between who she was at sixteen and who she was now seemed to her the distance between the earth and the moon.

Marvelle and Dick got up and stood at the edge of the lookout, Marvelle not going quite so close this time.

"It's romantic up here, isn't it?" Lawson said quietly to Holly.

"Kind of, but I think romantic is more like a state of mind."

"Why don't we go there?" Lawson said, his face turned toward Holly's, which was how he missed the bright shooting star that Holly, Marvelle, and Dick suddenly exclaimed over.

"I'm always missing things," Lawson said. "I've been that way all my life."

"You feel too fucking sorry for yourself," Marvelle told him.

Lawson sat up. He looked so forlorn that Holly reached up and patted his back.

"Thank you for pointing that out to me," he said to Marvelle. "I'll have to remember that. You've been a big help."

"You're welcome," Marvelle said.

They watched the sky for almost an hour without seeing another meteor. Holly was still lying on her back, and now and then Lawson stroked her hair. It felt so good that she couldn't bring herself to tell him to stop. After all, she thought, it wasn't his fault that she wished his hand belonged to someone else, or that, despite his interest in her, she felt lonely. When he moved his hand down to her shoulder and then her breast, she started to unbutton her blouse. But then Dick said, "Let's go. I don't think anything else is going to happen tonight."

They got in the car and headed back toward Venus. Lawson seemed to be struggling with his seat belt. "Darn it," he said to Holly. "This thing doesn't want to keep me away from you." He slid over and started to embrace her.

"Lawson," Holly said, more loudly than she'd meant to. He slowly moved back to his side of the seat.

After a while he said, "I have to put a German shepherd to sleep tomorrow. She's afraid of thunder. She jumps through windows. If you're alone," he said then, specifically to Holly, "there's not a lonelier sound in the world than thunder."

"Isn't that the truth," Dick said.

"Let me have her," Marvelle told Lawson. "I have dogs to keep her company."

"You've got her," Lawson said.

They were practically the only car on the highway. Trucks roared past them, one after the other, speeding. In the backseat, Holly felt Lawson looking at her. She kept her eyes on the back of Dick's head.

They passed the road that led to Marvelle's house, and soon after that the truck stop came into view, with its big, lit-up sign. Holly got her car keys from her purse; when Dick drove into the parking lot and stopped next to her car, Lawson leaned over and kissed her on the mouth. "I'll see you soon," he told her.

She and Marvelle got into the Chevette. "Maybe I should tell him to stop doing that," Holly said.

Marvelle didn't say anything. Then, when they were on the highway, driving west, she said, "I kissed Franklin Sanders once." She didn't look at Holly. "It was almost ten years ago, on a Sunday afternoon at church. I was helping some of the women decorate for Christmas. Franklin and I just happened to go into the kitchen at the same time, and suddenly we were kissing. That's how quickly it happened. Like we were helpless all of a sudden."

"Why didn't you ever tell me?" Holly said.

"It was private. I couldn't talk about it."

Marvelle looked out the window at the highway. "Now it seems so long ago." She put her hands on the dashboard as if a car or a deer might materialize in front of them.

"I drank too much," she said then. "Why did you let me drink so much?"

"When have I ever been able to stop you from doing anything?"

"I had a good time for a while, though, didn't I?" Marvelle asked. "Wasn't I laughing at one point?"

Holly left the highway, crossed Black Creek, and drove through the woods. She turned into Marvelle's long driveway. At the house, lights were on in the living room and the curtains were open; Curtis was sprawled on the couch, watching television.

"There he is," Marvelle said sadly, "right where we left him six hours ago."

$\mathcal{I}$t was after midnight by the time Holly got home. There were two calls on her answering machine: one from Owen, asking if he could bring Crystal over for dinner; and one from Reese Nyles, who sounded so much like Gene Rollison, at first, that Holly was dialing Gene's number when she heard Reese say, "Could you find out if Lawson Dyer knows where Jenny is?"

She put the phone down. Gene probably wasn't home, anyway, she thought. It was a Saturday night; he was probably on a date with someone. Holly imagined calling him anyway, to tell him about the meteor shower. She thought he was the kind of person who'd be interested in things like stars and planets, in more than just himself and his own small life. Though it didn't seem small to Holly; nothing about life did, anymore. People's lives were like that shooting star, she thought—too brief and unbelievably bright, though while you lived your life the brightness seemed to be outside yourself; the light seemed to be reflecting off of everyone else but you.

9

Three weeks later, on a muggy Friday afternoon in late June, Holly shopped in preparation for the dinner she was making Owen and Crystal that night. She was in the Food World parking lot, next to her car, when she saw Curtis drive by and call out to Wendy Dell, whose car was parked near Holly's. Wendy was retrieving empty Coke bottles from her trunk, and Curtis got out to talk to her. "Where have you been?" Holly heard him say. "I've been leaving messages for a week."

"I've been busy," Wendy told him.

"Busy with who?" Curtis said.

"That's just like you," Wendy said, "to jump to that con-clusion. All right. I might as well get this over with. There's somebody else in my life now." She said something else, in a quieter voice, that Holly couldn't hear.

Curtis had one foot up on the bumper of Wendy's car—he was wearing his pointy cowboy boots. Holly watched him remove it and take a step back. "Who is it?" he said coldly.

"I don't think that's important," Wendy told him.

"You don't?" Curtis said. "You don't think that's important?"

He was talking loudly and slowly. "Fuck you," he said. He walked around to the driver's side of his faded van with the parachute jumper painted on the side.

Holly left her groceries in the cart and went over to his van. "I know this is none of my business," she told him through his open window, "but I heard what Wendy said. I wanted to make sure you were all right."

Curtis looked at her. For a second, Holly had the feeling that he might do anything—hit her, get out and run, drive a hundred miles an hour through the parking lot. But a moment later he looked as stunned as Morgan had sometimes looked when he wasn't expecting to see anyone he knew.

"Why wouldn't I be all right?" he said. Then he started his van and wove his way quickly through the unevenly spaced parked cars. He hit a shopping cart and sent it rolling into a freshly waxed Cadillac.

*H*olly loaded her groceries and drove home. When she pulled up in front of her house, Lawson was sitting on the steps of his clinic. He came over and helped her carry things in.

"I was just thinking about you," he said. "You drove up in the middle of my thoughts."

"I didn't mean to," Holly said.

"I was thinking about the night we drove up to Pinnacle Mountain," Lawson told her. "Did I tell you that Dick and I went into my backyard later and saw ten or more meteors?" He put the grocery sacks on the kitchen counter. He took off his white clinical coat. "I thought about calling you, but Dick said you were probably in bed already."

"I was," Holly said.

"That made me want to call you even more."

Holly stopped putting perishables in the refrigerator. "Don't say that," she told Lawson. "I'm not interested in a relationship right now. And you of all people don't need to be hurt again."

"When do you think you will be interested?"

"Well, never," Holly told him. "Not with you, anyway." She closed the refrigerator door. "I mean, I don't have those kinds of feelings for you."

"You kissed me like you did."

"Did I?" Holly said. "Well, you had on that nice cologne."

"You started to unbutton your blouse out at Pinnacle Point," Lawson said.

"I stopped, though. I didn't get far enough for you to actually see anything."

"You like me more than you want to admit."

"I don't think so," Holly said. "But I like you as a neighbor, Lawson. I think we're good at being neighbors."

"You're right," he said. "We're excellent neighbors, which is how I know we're meant for each other."

"We're not meant for each other."

"Sure we are."

"I may be wrong," Holly said, "but isn't this something people need to agree on?"

"I agree enough for both of us," Lawson said.

Holly laughed. "I don't think it works that way," she told him, "but I don't have time right now to talk about it. Can't we talk about this some other time?"

"Absolutely," he said. "Good. That's all I ask." He picked up his lab coat and touched her shoulder before opening the kitchen door. Holly watched from her window as he stepped through a gap in her forsythia bushes and moved quickly across his yard. He was slender and not much taller than she was, but at that moment Holly had the impression that he could have walked right through the walls of his clinic if he'd wanted to.

She put away the rest of her groceries and called Marvelle.

"Wendy broke up with Curtis in the Food World parking lot," she told her.

Marvelle was silent for a long moment. "That explains an argument we just had about nothing. I wish he could have told me."

"Could have?" Holly said. "Well, he could have if he'd wanted to."

"No," Marvelle said. "He doesn't know how to talk about his feelings. He's just like Morgan." She was silent again. Holly thought she could feel, even over the telephone, how afraid Marvelle was but then decided she was wrong; Marvelle told her, in a more cheerful voice, about Hoyt, the German shepherd Lawson had given her. She said that Hoyt was learning to sleep on the sixty-five-dollar dog bed she'd gotten mail order from L. L. Bean.

"It's difficult for him," she told Holly. "He's not used to something so cushiony. It takes him a long time to settle down."

They hung up, and Holly stood at the kitchen sink, rinsing lettuce. She watched two crows fly over her yard and disappear into Lawson's flowering apricot tree. He had a lot more luck with trees than he did with women, Holly thought.

She got serious about cooking. She was making broiled chicken breasts, steamed vegetables, and a salad with Paul Newman dressing. The only thing Crystal could fault her for, she thought, was buying packaged chicken at the store rather than driving out into the country to find people who raised, apologized to, and slaughtered chickens themselves.

She set the table in her dining area—a small corner of her living room that was brightened by a window overlooking her garden. Outside, the sky was dark with storm clouds. She could see the silver undersides of the leaves. She went into her bedroom and changed her clothes three times— from jeans to slacks to the black dress she'd worn to Morgan's funeral. She thought it made her look thinner and more fit.

$\mathcal{O}$wen and Crystal arrived at six o'clock; Crystal was wearing a white cotton dress and sandals. Owen had on jeans and a striped shirt, and he'd had his hair cut more fashionably.

"It just started to rain," Crystal said, "like about a second ago. Maybe that will cool things off." She pushed back her straight brown hair and long bangs. She wore glasses, which had slid down a little on her small nose.

"Crystal doesn't like real hot days—it's harder for her to run then," Owen explained.

"I still do it, though," Crystal said. "You can't get hung up on a thing like the weather. You have to push yourself through that barrier."

Owen and Crystal sat down on the red sofa Holly had bought at an auction in Ferrisville. A mouse had jumped out of it as she and Owen carried it into the house, and now, looking at her son sitting so close to his former sixth-grade teacher, Holly found herself wishing another mouse would appear, so that Owen and Crystal would feel as surprised and uncomfortable as she did.

"Would you like something to drink?" Holly asked them.

"Wine sounds awesome to me, Mom," Owen said.

"Yes, it does," Holly told him, "but I didn't buy any. I'm sorry. I thought that since you're only sixteen, we would all drink fruit juice."

"Fruit juice is a healthier choice, anyway," Crystal said.

Holly went into the kitchen for the drinks, and when she came back out Owen had moved to the floor and was sitting at Crystal's feet. "What's for dinner, Mom?" he asked.

"Broiled chicken breasts," she said.

"With the skin on or off?"

"Off," Holly told him. "Just the opposite of the way you used to like them."

"Owen's learning to eat healthier foods," Crystal told Holly. "I don't think he realized how much fat was in his diet."

"Is that right?" Holly said to Owen. "Even though I used to tell you every day?"

"I was only fifteen then," Owen said.

"He's grown up a lot," Crystal told Holly. "Sometimes people just mature all at once, for no apparent reason." She put her hand on Owen's dark hair.

Right then, Holly had a memory of herself at Owen's age—her parents discovering her half-naked, with Burke, on top of the clothes dryer in the basement. *Mature* was one of the words she had used that night to defend herself.

"I think dinner's ready," Holly said. She escaped into the kitchen, swallowed a mouthful of vodka from the bottle she kept in the freezer, and brought the food into the dining room. Owen and Crystal were sitting down at the table.

"It's been a while since I've had anyone over for dinner except Owen," Holly told Crystal. "I usually just eat dinner at work."

"I come over here whenever I see Annette getting out her Chinese cookbook," Owen said.

"Chinese food is wonderful," Crystal told him, "though it can be high in fat."

"That's what I mean," Owen said quickly. "I get out of there before the lard starts flying."

Outside, it began to storm. Flashes of lightning lit up the wall behind Crystal's head. "Wow, you look great," Owen told her. "Like some kind of monster in a science-fiction movie."

"Owen," Holly said.

"I know what he means," Crystal told Holly. "Owen and I both like science fiction. I told him he might want to try writing it himself, someday, maybe in college."

Holly looked at Owen, who was carefully cutting off a speck of chicken skin she had missed. "You're going to college?" she asked him.

"Sure," Owen said. "Why not?"

Crystal helped herself to more vegetables and smiled at Holly. It was still thundering outside; the curtains were open and Holly could see the rain falling on her garden. Across the table from her, Owen was eating salad eagerly for the first time in her memory.

After they'd finished dinner, Crystal excused herself to use the rest room. Holly and Owen cleared the table.

"Didn't you want to quit high school a few months ago?" Holly asked him.

"I don't think so," Owen said.

"Well, good," Holly told him. "I'm glad I'm remembering it wrong. But if you really want to go to college, you should start earning something higher than C's and D's."

"That's the good part," Owen said. "Crystal says that all I need to get into the University of Kansas is a high school diploma."

"You might want to stay in, though," Holly said.

She served fruit for dessert, and herbal tea, and then, while Owen was in the kitchen, washing dishes—he'd jumped at the chance because Crystal suggested it—Crystal and Holly sat together in the living room, Crystal on the couch again, Holly in the armchair her mother had given her.

"Thank you for dinner," Crystal said. "I told Owen how stressful this would be for you, but I think you're handling it real well. I bet even you're surprised."

"Surprised is how I felt when I saw the two of you outside your apartment building," Holly told her angrily; she'd just remembered how Crystal had lied to her at the Hearth.

"But don't you think it's good for people to be shaken up sometimes?" Crystal asked.

"No," Holly said. She got up and opened the door and looked out; the rain had stopped. "What I worry about," she said, without turning around, "is what will happen when you meet someone you like who's your own age."

"That won't happen," Crystal said. "At least it doesn't have to."

"It usually does, though," Holly said.

Owen came in then, wiping his hands on his jeans. "Why don't you buy a dishwasher, Mom?" he said. "Wouldn't that be a lot easier?"

*H*olly walked out onto the porch with them. They were holding hands. In the last year Owen had grown almost as tall and broad-shouldered as his father, but instead of Burke's fleshy face he had Holly's father's prominent cheekbones and dark eyes.

"Good night now," Crystal called out as she unlocked her car door for Owen. She was standing beneath the leaves of Lawson's sweet gum tree, which shaded part of Holly's yard; her white dress was the only part of her visible. In the wet air it looked almost luminescent. After Crystal and Owen drove away, Holly picked off the dead blooms of the potted geraniums on her porch and listened to an owl calling from somewhere. She and Marvelle had seen one two nights earlier, perched high in the oak tree next to Morgan's garage—Marvelle's garage now, Holly knew, and Curtis's, but it was hard for her to think of it that way.

Inside she cleaned up what Owen hadn't—the top of the stove, the sink, bits of lettuce on the floor. She ended up washing the floor, not because it was dirty, but because it gave her something to do besides thinking about Owen and Crystal. She'd thought about them all day—especially, she realized now, after she saw Wendy Dell break up with Curtis in the parking lot. It was terrible to fool yourself about love, Holly thought. It was like discovering you'd mortgaged your future up to the hilt to buy a house with a sinking foundation.

It was almost ten o'clock. She carried the trash out to the garbage cans. Lawson's Cherokee was out front, and lights were on in his clinic. Holly had almost forgotten about the conversation they'd had earlier. Before, in her life, she'd have done almost anything, including getting married, to keep someone from feeling rejected or brokenhearted. Now she didn't worry so much about people's hearts. They seemed to heal, or not to—like Morgan's—but not because of what other people did or didn't do. Holly felt that "heartbroken" was an exaggeration, anyway. She was starting to believe, lately, that people might be better off paying attention to what they thought instead of what they felt, since a brain was at least a real thing. No one thought it stood for anything else.

Holly locked her doors and turned off her lights. Lying in bed, she heard the owl call; she heard Lawson start his Cherokee and rainwater drip from the eaves, and after that, beginning to dream, she imagined unconnected things, one after the other. They settled into a dream that made more sense than life, because so many odd and random things seemed reasonable, and fit together.

10

The Fourth of July was hot by eight in the morning, when Holly got up and watered her flowers. By the time she drove to work at ten-thirty, the bank sign said ninety-nine degrees. Will was opening the Hearth for lunch in order to take advantage of the parade watchers.

Holly parked behind the restaurant before the parade started. The high school band and drill team were lined up half a block away, and as she got out of her car she heard the bandleader yell into a megaphone, "I better not see any of that condom business from last year. Those of you responsible know what I'm talking about. The rest of you people—stay on my good side."

In the kitchen Cleveland had just taken a sheet cake out of the oven, and Sue-Ellis was decorating it with stars and stripes. Marvelle was tacking up red, white, and blue streamers in the doorway between the kitchen and the dining room.

"This heat is going to make us money," Will said as he walked quickly through the kitchen. He seemed nervous to Holly, which she understood when she went into the dining room and saw that his wife and four children were sitting at a window table, waiting for the parade to come by. The kids were drinking Cokes and eating plates of french fries. Evelyn was smoking. Holly watched Will bring her an ashtray and tell the children not to touch the window with their ketchupy fingers.

Back in the kitchen, while Holly filled a tray of glasses with ice, Sue-Ellis said, "I want to see the baton twirlers. I still have my baton from junior high. Sometimes I go out in my backyard at night and practice."

"You're kidding," Cleveland said.

"You know I'm not." Sue-Ellis showed Holly how she'd put her initials at the very bottom of the cake, in the center of a white stripe. "I paint a little at home," she told Holly. "I watch that public-television program where the artist shows you how to do clouds and trees."

Will hurried back into the kitchen. "Cleveland, can you make my wife a grilled cheese with tomato, and grill the tomato separately before you put it on the sandwich? You know how she likes it."

"I know exactly," Cleveland said. "And I know she'll send it back no matter how good it is."

"Let's worry about that when it happens," Will said.

The parade had started. Holly, Marvelle, and Sue-Ellis went through the dining room and out the front door to watch. They stood on the sidewalk as eight baton twirlers passed by in their blue-tasseled tops and red skirts, and then the band, several of whom—mostly drummers—were displaying colored condoms on their fingers. Following the band and preceding the fire engine were the little girls from the LaMere School of Dance, pirouetting in front of a white convertible that belonged to Gerald LaMere, who was standing up in the backseat, waving. Holly waved back; she'd taken dancing classes from him when she was a child.

Will had been wrong to stay open, Holly thought at first, when the parade was over and only a few customers trickled in—among them Gene Rollison, who sat in Sue-Ellis's section. When Holly walked past his booth, she heard Sue-Ellis say to him, "Even when you have long legs, like I do, it's still a bitch to weave it in and out between them."

"I didn't know you knew Gene," Holly said to her a few minutes later in the kitchen.

"Gene and I go way back," Sue-Ellis said, "though only in a business capacity. He arrested my first husband—twice, I think."

"He's a well-meaning person," Marvelle told her.

"Is he?" Sue-Ellis said. "I hope so. I invited him over for dinner tonight. I thought he was hinting at it. He said, 'I wish I could cook as well as Cleveland Harris.'" She picked up the coffeepot. "I know it doesn't sound like much, but you can't expect men to say what they mean. That would be like asking fish to talk."

"Maybe you've known the wrong men," Holly told her.

"There's no question about that," Sue-Ellis said.

The bell on the front door was ringing, and when Holly looked in the dining room she discovered a line of sweaty, impatient people, and more customers coming in behind them. The tables filled up and there were still people waiting. Holly, Sue-Ellis, Marvelle, the busperson Will had hired that morning, and even Will ran around distributing drinks and taking orders, which ended up all coming in at once; the kitchen backed up and Cleveland began swearing. Out in the dining room, two of Will's children were crying. Holly brought all four kids ice cream to quiet them down. Will was yelling at them, which wasn't helping.

"Goddamn it," he said to Holly over a dirty table they were quickly trying to clear and reset. "I'm tired of listening to my kids cry and my wife complain."

"It's not like Evelyn held a gun to your head to get those children," Holly said.

"Don't take your bad mood out on me," Will snapped at her. "I'm just as busy as you are."

At the next table, Reese Nyles was looking at Holly and pointing to his empty coffee cup; at a window booth, Lawson Dyer and Dick Spearman were waving their menus at her.

The air conditioner quit working.

"I can only take so much pressure," Sue-Ellis said to Will in the kitchen as he and Holly were piling eight of their or-ders—finally ready—on a big tray. "I'm going to smack one of my customers. He has it coming."

"You're not smacking anybody," Will said. "Get hold of yourself. Feed him and get rid of him."

"Get your hands off that meatloaf," Cleveland shouted at Marvelle. "It's not yours. What makes you think every plate of meat loaf is yours?"

The busperson, a tired-looking sixteen-year-old girl, was standing in a corner, crying.

Finally, after all the customers had gotten their food, eaten, complained about the service, and left, Will locked the door and came back into the kitchen. The busperson had been sent home. The air conditioner, which had begun to work again in fits and starts, was emitting lukewarm, musty-smelling air.

"I'm the one to take the blame, here," Will said. "I should have taken on extra help."

"That's for sure," Sue-Ellis said.

"Could you be gracious for once? I just admitted this was my fault."

"Why should I congratulate you for being right about how wrong you were?" Sue-Ellis said.

"Because it's the polite thing to do," Will told her. "You take this honesty crap too far."

Cleveland brought his fist down on the counter, which put an end to the conversation. He weighed two hundred and fifty pounds. "I'd like to make a suggestion," he said. "Let's eat my flag cake." It was still intact; no one had ordered it. He got out plates and forks and served everyone an evenly sized square.

"I'd like a star, please," Sue-Ellis said.

*H*olly left the restaurant at three o'clock, irritable and sweaty. Marvelle was already out back; she'd parked her pickup next to the trash bin and was throwing cardboard cups and old magazines into it. "Look what I found under the seat," she told Holly, holding up a small pocket knife. "Morgan lost this a year ago."

"Give it to Curtis," Holly said.

"I don't think so. I'm going to take it out to the cemetery and bury it under the flowers."

Holly watched Marvelle get in her pickup and speed across the gravel into the street—in a hurry, as usual. Marvelle always drove fast; she'd met Gene, Holly knew, when he stopped her and gave her a ticket. Holly, herself, had always had the bad luck to be law-abiding.

She started her own car, the inside of which, she guessed, was about a hundred and thirty degrees. She opened the windows, turned the air conditioner on high, and drove home. Then she walked into her house, undressed, and fell asleep on her couch.

*I*t was almost seven when she awoke. She showered, dressed, and took a glass of iced tea out to her porch. The sun was low in the hazy sky; it was hard for Holly to believe it was the same sun that had blazed down on Venus all day.

Marvelle drove up as Holly was sitting there. She walked across the yard up to the house.

"You were at the cemetery all this time?" Holly asked. "What were you doing?"

"Sitting and thinking." Marvelle sat down on Holly's steps.

"Your eyes are red," Holly told her. She handed Marvelle the glass of tea and watched a blue jay fly in and out of Lawson's sweet gum tree. "I don't think it's good for you to spend so much time out there. It's not healthy."

"Oh. Like you know what's healthy," Marvelle said. "You're the one who wanted to live next to that cemetery." She drank the rest of Holly's iced tea. "Anyway, I got to see Gene drive up to Sue-Ellis's house for dinner."

"Oh, great," Holly said.

"I didn't feel anything," Marvelle said.

Neither of them had eaten dinner, and they went inside, into the kitchen, where Holly made tuna-fish sandwiches. "Was Gene dressed up?" she asked Marvelle. "Was he wearing a tie?"

"I don't think so. Why?"

"I just wondered. I can't believe he's interested in Sue-Ellis. Just about anyone would be happy to go out with him."

"Well, she knows those baton tricks," Marvelle said. "And she makes the first move. Men like to feel wanted, Holly. They like to be taken seriously."

"What do you mean?" Holly said.

"I mean, they're not all jerks. They want to love somebody, just like we do."

Marvelle ate the last bite of her sandwich and got up to walk around Holly's small kitchen. "I can't seem to sit still anymore, Holly. I feel restless everywhere except the cemetery. I think I'm starting to feel a little the way you do, thinking about death and everything."

"That's not fair," Holly said. "I was only like that after my father died, just for a year or so, and then maybe I get that way once in a while, when I get depressed about life, or hear some bad news."

"Or start worrying about Owen," Marvelle said, "or a dream you had, or that you might be sick, or that your mother might be sick, or your stepfather, or me, or somebody else you know, or somebody you don't know but heard about." Marvelle stopped to take a breath.

"So?" Holly said.

Marvelle didn't answer. She looked at Holly, looked at a clipping on Holly's refrigerator—WOMAN DIES FROM RARE SPIDER BITE—then looked outside at the pale, early-evening sky. The refrigerator started up. A car down the street backfired.

"Let's go see the fireworks," Marvelle told Holly. "We'll drive out to my house first so that I can change clothes."

"You should have changed out of that uniform earlier," Holly said. "You can get a rash from wearing sweaty clothes."

*O*n their way out of town, Holly saw a few premature fireworks—illegal ones people were setting off in their yards. Most of them were going off over the Acres of Trailers Park; they were probably Burke's, Holly thought. He liked them because they were dangerous. He liked narrow escapes, moments when things could explode or not, kill you or not. He liked to be scared and for other people to be, too. For the first time Holly was glad that Owen was almost always, these days, at Crystal's apartment. Every year she worried about him getting hurt. And for good reason, she felt like telling Marvelle—some of the things she worried about were real.

The sun was setting as Marvelle sped down the highway. "Look at the cranes," she said as they drove over Black Creek, and Holly saw two of them fly low over the water and up and over the cottonwood trees.

At Marvelle's house, Curtis was standing outside the garage, feeding the hunting dogs. "I just painted the Triumph fenders," Curtis told his mother. "The fumes are strong as hell in there."

"Where's Hoyt?" Marvelle asked him.

"In the house." Curtis walked away, across the gravel. He had on jeans, boots, and a worn T-shirt, and his long hair was tied back with string.

"I hope he's had his dinner," Marvelle said.

"He's thirty-one years old," Holly told her. "He's old enough to take care of himself."

"I meant Hoyt." Marvelle headed for the house, calling the dog's name even before she had the door open.

Holly waited for her outside. The pearl-colored sky was darkening, and she stood under the oak tree next to the garage, looking out at the ravine. She was hoping to hear the owl call and be able to see it. What she heard instead was Curtis, coming around the back of the garage.

"Jesus Christ," he said when he saw her. "You scared the shit out of me."

"My father used to say that," Holly told him. "I'd scare him just walking into the living room, like he didn't remember I lived there."

"I thought you were in the house with my mother," Curtis said.

Neither of them spoke, until Holly, to break the silence, said, "Did you see the parade this morning?"

"I drove in too late."

"What did you do in town?"

"I didn't see Wendy, if that's what you mean."

"I didn't mean anything," Holly told him. "I was just being friendly."

"Oh," Curtis said. He looked away from her. "I wasn't trying to be rude."

You don't have to try, Holly thought, but she said, "I probably shouldn't have come up to you that day in the parking lot. It was none of my business."

"I was embarrassed," Curtis told her; he took a step back toward the wooded ravine.

Holly looked at his profile—his face not as thin as Morgan's had been, his skin healthier, his eyes lighter.

"I would have been embarrassed, too," Holly said, and then, "Why don't you come with us to see the fireworks?"

"Now?" Curtis looked at his watch, which had been Morgan's, Holly knew; she was relieved that it didn't get buried along with the pocket knife. "Maybe I will," he said.

*M*arvelle drove and Holly sat in the middle. They took the highway back into Venus and then turned onto Ferrisville Road; the fireworks were at the high school football field.

"Half the fireworks were duds last year," Curtis told them. "Dad said Venus got ripped off."

"I don't remember Dad being with us," Marvelle said.

"He drove out in his jeep and watched from halfway up the water tower." Curtis shifted his long legs, giving Holly more room. "He told me that a week later."

"Dad had a secretive streak," Marvelle said.

"Yeah, maybe," Curtis said, and looked out the window. Holly kept her eyes on her lap, feeling out of place, and was relieved when Marvelle pulled into the parking lot, sunbursts and Roman candles exploding above them. Marvelle said they might as well stay in the truck to watch; she didn't think there were any parking places left, anyway.

"Well, I'm getting out and walking around," Holly said.

Curtis got out to let her out. "I'll come with you," he told her. He followed her across the parking lot and into the football field. He was watching the fireworks as he walked, and he stumbled into her a few times, which was partly her fault. She was looking up as well, and remembering that when she was a child she and her father would go see the fireworks by themselves each year—her mother hadn't liked the loud noise or the mosquitoes.

Back then the high school hadn't been built yet, and the fireworks took place at the community park south of Venus, where a discount store was now. The drive there and back would be unpredictable—her father might talk the whole time or not at all. During the fireworks he would maneuver her around, trying to find the best place for them to sit. He didn't hold her hand, which would have been the easiest thing. He kept his hand just behind her back, not touching her as long as she kept up, lightly pushing her forward when she didn't. The trick, it seemed to Holly even then, was to touch her as little as possible. He was always like that. When she got sick or hurt, he worried more than he needed to, but when she was the healthy child she usually was, there was a river of space between them. Holly had sometimes imagined her mother as a boat that went back and forth between her father and the unappealing bank that was herself.

Now, Holly noticed Gene Rollison and Sue-Ellis ahead of her, standing a little apart from each other, and Holly accidentally bumped into Gene when Curtis walked into her once more, stepping so hard on her heel that her shoe came off. "Sorry," Curtis said.

"It's all right," she told him. She put her shoe back on, balancing herself on the steadying arm Gene held out to her.

11

The hot weather continued throughout July, along with a dry wind that blew constantly. Toward the end of the month, Will Chaffe started calling Holly late at night from home; he called her at one in the morning on the Friday of her thirty-sixth birthday.

"Are you waking me up so that I'll look even older to myself in the morning?" she asked him. Outside she heard the wind tearing up the wind chime in her crab apple tree.

"I just wanted to be the first person to wish you happy birthday," he said.

In the morning, Marvelle took her out for breakfast and to the mall in Ferrisville, so that she could pick out her own birthday present. Holly burst into tears at the cosmetics counter; the young clerk had suggested she buy products

from their "over thirty-five line." After that, Holly and Marvelle wandered through the mall for two hours.

"It's not that I don't see things I like," Holly said. "It's that
I don't see things that would look good on me anymore."
They left without buying anything and walked across the
street to have margaritas and enchiladas at La Fiesta.

"Why shouldn't I buy makeup for people over thirty-
five?" Holly said later, on the drive back to Venus. "I've been
over thirty-five for a year. I don't know what's wrong with
me." She looked out the window at the parched grass and the
dry fields, which didn't even seem to attract crows anymore.

"I just don't like that word, *moisturizer,*" she told Marvelle.

*A*t home, Hoyt was sleeping on Holly's shady porch, where
Marvelle had left him tied up. Marvelle was putting his water
bowl down in front of him when Lawson came over from
next door and told them that Dick Spearman had had a heart
attack that morning.

"A mild one," Lawson said. "He's at Martin County Hospital. I'm on my way out there now."

"It's one thing after another, isn't it?" Marvelle said.

"It's really depressing," Holly said.

"Well, he's not dead," Lawson told them. "He's doing
okay. I called his mother, who's coming down from Iowa. I
couldn't talk her out of it."

"Let's all drive to the hospital together," Marvelle said. "We
won't feel better until we see him." She insisted on taking
Hoyt with them; she put him in the backseat, with Lawson,
while she herself sat up front with Holly, who was driving.

"Does Dick smoke?" Marvelle asked, once they were on their way.

"Sometimes," Lawson said.

"I had a feeling he did," Marvelle said. "And there's all that fast food he eats. I tried to tell him that."

"I think it's the stress of being alone that does it," Lawson said.

They left Venus behind, heading north. They drove past the landfill and through Hardin and Waverly, and then through open country. The worst heat of the day was finally behind them. The hospital was forty minutes from Venus; Holly had forgotten it was so far. She hadn't been there since her father died. As she drove, she kept catching sight of Hoyt's intelligent face in her rearview mirror. The dog seemed so human that more than once she'd been on the verge of saying to him, "Excuse me," or "Is there anything I can get you?" That was practically the way Marvelle spoke to him. Right now Marvelle was turned around in her seat, saying to Hoyt, "We'll be there before long, sweetheart. Then you can get out and pee."

At the hospital, Holly parked in the shade, and Marvelle took Hoyt for a brief walk. Then she, Holly, and Lawson went inside and up in the clean, quiet elevator to the cardiac floor. When they got to Dick's room, he was sitting up in bed, looking pale, watching a game show on television. Before he'd had time to say much of anything, a nurse came in and said visitors would be more welcome tomorrow. She said that Lawson could stay, however; he'd lied and said he was Dick's brother. Holly and Marvelle went out and sat in the small waiting area.

"Poor Dick," Holly said. "That's what I keep thinking."

"Poor Dick could have chewed gum and eaten chicken like the rest of us," Marvelle told her. She got up to look out the window. They were on the fourth floor, overlooking the parking area and beyond that a cluster of one-story medical buildings. Two nurses were at the desk down the corridor. Holly picked up a magazine and read an article called "Aging with Beauty."

Lawson came out after half an hour. "Dick's comfortable, physically," he said. "They're going to do tests tomorrow, and he's scheduled for an angiogram Monday morning. They think he'll probably need angioplasty." He stood with Marvelle for a moment at the window. "That's a procedure to unclog an artery."

"We know what it is," Marvelle said. "We read. We watch TV."

They went down in the elevator and walked out of the hospital into the warm early evening. Marvelle took Hoyt over to the grass in front of the medical buildings while Holly and Lawson waited next to the car. They could see a small lake across the highway.

"We could all be in the same boat Dick is," Lawson said. "In the hospital without a loved one."

"Didn't you say his mother was driving down here tomorrow?" Holly asked.

"I'm not talking about a mother," Lawson said. "I'm talking about a spouse or a lover—somebody who would be with him now and rush back here first thing in the morning." He touched Holly's arm. "None of us are getting any younger."

Holly watched Marvelle walk Hoyt back and wait patiently while he delicately lifted his leg at each light post.

"Why don't we take you to the nursing home now?" Holly said to Lawson. "What's the point of waiting forty years?"

"I seem to have touched a nerve," Lawson said. Holly didn't say another word until they were all in the car, driving home on the highway. Then she asked Lawson to please remove Hoyt's cold nose from the back of her neck; it was giving her the creeps.

*W*aiting at home for Holly on the front porch was a birthday package: a white summer robe from her mother, and from her stepfather a pair of gardening gloves and a magazine article from *Today's Hygiene* about germs in soil that can infect people through microscopic abrasions on their hands. In the mail was a card from Owen, also signed with Crystal's name—the two of them had left three days earlier for a camping trip in the Ozarks. And there was a card from Holly's insurance agent, reminding her that it was never too soon to acquire life insurance.

After dark, Holly sat on her porch in her new robe, looking at the fireflies and thinking about how, if she were a different kind of person, she'd celebrate her birthday by getting drunk and digging around in her garden with her bare hands. Despite being raised by a reckless father, and marrying Burke, and having an affair with a married man, she'd somehow ended up a cowardly person. She knew that. She wouldn't take even mild chances, and was terrified of really dangerous

things, like mountain climbing, or parachute jumping, or—
she thought now—picking up the phone, calling Gene Rollison, and saying, "I'm aging. Can you come over?"

She forced herself to go to bed that night without brushing her teeth, and she woke up at two from a dream in which
her teeth had fallen out. She got out of bed and brushed.

$\mathcal{H}$olly and Marvelle went back to see Dick in the morning.
It was Marvelle's idea. "I couldn't sleep," she told Holly on
the way there, in her pickup. "I thought about how rude I
used to be to Dick, making jokes about his sperm and all, and
how I wasn't very friendly."

On the seat, between them, Franklin Sanders's *Grieving
with God* cassette was still wrapped in plastic. Holly noticed
that a cassette called *Loving Your Dog* was in the tape player.
Marvelle was driving at her usual rapid pace; they were bar-
reling down the highway past the landfill. After that were
wheat fields on both sides of the road under the hot sky. The
wind had stopped, and the humidity had risen. For the first
time in three weeks there was no motion anywhere, which
looked odd to Holly. She had the feeling they were driving
through a painting.

They went into the crowded hospital cafeteria for breakfast
and spotted Franklin Sanders ahead of them in line. He
smiled and waved at them.

"I wish I could tell if he's happy to see me or if he just wants
to talk me into coming back to church," Marvelle said. She
watched Franklin carry his tray to a vacant table. "He looks
tired to me," she said to Holly. "Does he look tired to you?"

"Dick Spearman is on my list of people to see," Franklin said when they joined him and mentioned Dick's name. "I visit anyone who's not Catholic, Jewish, Jehovah's Witness, or Muslim. That's the way the clergy divides it up." Franklin broke the yolks of his eggs.

"Doesn't your wife tell you not to eat those?" Marvelle said to him. She had gotten a bran muffin, a banana, and juice.

"I can't keep track of all the things my wife tells me not to do, but no, she's never mentioned eggs."

Marvelle stood up, picked up his plate, and walked back to the cafeteria line. She returned with a bowl of oatmeal and low-fat milk.

"Am I supposed to say thank you?" Franklin asked.

"Only if you want to be polite."

He opened the milk and poured it on the cereal. "This might be a good subject for Sunday's sermon," he told them. "Sometimes real kindness is not giving people what they want."

"Feel free to use it," Marvelle said.

The three of them rode up in the elevator to Dick's floor. A man behind Holly was wheezing slightly; someone else was quietly counting aloud the floor numbers. Franklin, who was standing behind Marvelle, put his hands on her shoulders for just a moment to steady her when the elevator jolted to a stop.

Dick's mother had already arrived and was in Dick's room; she'd driven down the day before. "I wanted to see my boy just as soon as I could," she told them.

"I'll come back tomorrow afternoon or Monday," Franklin told Dick, but Holly and Marvelle stayed, listening to Dick's mother talk about her drive to Venus, the nice room she was staying in at Lawson's house, and Sioux City's placement on the "Ten Best Places to Live" list. After a while, Holly and Marvelle excused themselves and went down to the hospital gift shop.

"At least we can buy him something," Marvelle said. She was looking at religious medals hanging from silver chains. "It's no wonder Dick wants to kill himself—his mother took ten minutes to describe her breakfast."

"I don't think he wants to kill himself," Holly said. "I think he just likes pork."

Marvelle considered toilet articles, stuffed animals, and slippers, and finally bought Dick a book called *Your Healthy Heart*. She and Holly went back upstairs and tiptoed past Dick's roommate, an older man sleeping so heavily that Holly stopped at the foot of his bed.

"Can you tell if he's breathing?" she whispered to Marvelle.

"Stop thinking everybody's dead," Marvelle said.

But Holly didn't stop worrying until he turned over in his sleep. She didn't trust hospitals—she didn't like the way patients were treated like orphaned children, as if suddenly anything could be done to them. It seemed to Holly that if you were wearing a flimsy cotton gown and forced to stay in bed, the way Dick was, you should be treated with extra dignity, to make up for it.

"Honey, keep your feet under the covers," Dick's mother told him, "or else let me clip those toenails."

"What you want is bowel regularity and good circulation," Marvelle said, reading from the book she'd bought.

Dick was looking at his watch on the nightstand and seemed relieved when Holly said, "Why don't we all give Dick a chance to nap?"

*O*n the way home Marvelle stopped at the cemetery in order to water the flowers on Morgan's grave. Holly sat cross-legged in the grass and watched her fill up her big watering can and carry it over. The cemetery lawn was so dry it was crunchy, and large patches of it were turning brown. "This just breaks my heart," Marvelle said. "Using a little water out here isn't going to kill anyone."

From where Holly was sitting, she could see her father's grave at the bottom of the hill, right where Hope ended and Forgiveness began. On a cold November afternoon following her father's death, she'd run into Reese Nyles here, visiting the grave of his younger brother, who'd been killed years before in a jeep accident on an army base.

"I can never get over it," Reese told Holly that day. "I was the one in the war. I was the one in danger."

They walked through the cemetery together before getting into their separate cars, and Holly had sat there for a while, suddenly imagining herself and Reese as a couple. She didn't know why, even now, except that it had something to do with her father, and something to do with the way she looked at love—as if it were more about the past than the present, and more about death than life. She had sat there until the streetlights had come on. Then, reluctantly, she'd driven home to Burke and Owen.

Marvelle was weeding marigolds. The weather was changing; a dark bank of clouds was settling over Venus like a quilt.

"I just hate it when Morgan's bed looks scraggly," Marvelle said.

"His bed?" Holly asked.

"Flower bed," Marvelle told her, correcting herself.

*T*hat night it rained for the first time in a month. Holly had just gotten home early from working a slow dinner shift at the Hearth; Will had closed the restaurant at seven. Holly had a big grease stain on her uniform from Sue-Ellis running into her with a plate of pot roast. "I'm sorry," Sue-Ellis said to Holly. "Gene Rollison walked in, and I got excited."

"Forget it," Holly had said, but she was still angry as she undressed and showered and put on clean clothes. How could clumsy Sue-Ellis have ever been a dancer, Holly thought. Then she remembered going to the Truck City Bar once with Burke, and what the dancing had actually been like. Burke had asked her to do a similar dance for him after they got home, and Holly had tried—she'd put on high heels and the skimpy red outfit Burke had bought her for Valentine's Day. But it wasn't the same; Holly had been too self-conscious to move anything but her feet. A week later, she got drunk and performed more spontaneously, on top of the kitchen table, but somehow it was too late by then. Burke wasn't in the mood, anymore. Worse, she'd forgotten to close the kitchen blinds.

"What in the world were you doing, honey?" a neighbor had asked Holly the next day at the grocery store. "Some kind of aerobic housecleaning?"

Holly sat in her living room and listened to the rain and thunder. She absently touched the necklace Will had given her that evening for her birthday; he'd waylaid her in the laundry room and put it around her neck. Now her phone rang, and when Holly answered it, Will said, "I've left Evelyn. I'm at the Venus Motel in Room 107."

Holly put on a raincoat and ran out through the storm to her car. She drove slowly and carefully, not questioning why she was going, but not thinking about it either. Instead, she listened to the end of "Neighbor Talk" on the radio.

"I want a sermon tomorrow that I can relate to, Franklin," Gussie Dell said. "And Dick Spearman, I don't know you, but Venus expects anyone who gets sick here to get well immediately." She sang the first verse of "America, the Beautiful," before saying good night to her listeners and a special good night to her ailing sister: "I want you in bed within an hour, Beatrice, or I'll come over and put you there myself."

The Venus Motel was on the other side of town, on Highway 19, next to the drive-in movie theater that was no longer in operation. The motel was small and run-down, with a flat roof and cinder-block walls. Holly parked next to Will's car. She watched the rain pour off the motel roof and thought about how, when she was sixteen, she'd once seen her father's car parked almost exactly where hers was now. She'd never told a soul.

She opened the car door and ran through the rain to Will's room. The door was unlocked; he was sitting on the bed, waiting.

12

olly had only been in a dingier motel once, in Oklahoma City, when Burke had passed up a Super 8 and a Motel 6 to stop at a twelve-unit motel that advertised hot water and heat. Will's room at the Venus Motel was a little nicer than that, larger and more modern—there was even a television bolted to the wall—but the wallpaper was coming unglued and the green carpeting was stained. Will was sitting on the double bed, his face pale, his dark hair damp. Holly turned off the glaring overhead light and switched on the bedside lamp instead.

"Do I look that bad?" Will said.

"No, but the room does."

She sat on the bed with her back against the headboard and listened to him talk. He hadn't planned to leave, he said;

Holly knew that better than anyone, since if he was going to leave, why wouldn't he have left months ago, before Holly had stopped seeing him? Things had just happened, he said. Evelyn was unhappy and griping at him all the time; she lost her temper over just about anything he said or did. The kids were whinier when he was around, according to her. And tonight, when he got home from work, she threw a fit because he'd forgotten to bring home ice cream.

"And that was it," he said. "I went into the bedroom and packed a suitcase." He leaned back against the headboard, next to Holly. "If I'd given it any thought, it would have been the hardest thing I'd ever done. The only reason I could do it is because I didn't think."

Holly looked at his face in the light from the lamp. "You didn't do this for me, did you?" she asked.

"Yes," he said. And then, "No. Well, not for you. I did it because of you. I know the difference now between loving someone and not loving someone. I know the difference in how it feels."

There was a mirror on the opposite wall, above the bureau, and when Holly saw herself in it without expecting to she looked so serious she hardly recognized herself.

"You should go home," she told Will. "You shouldn't make a big decision like this all of a sudden."

"It was sudden and it wasn't sudden," Will said. The room was too warm, and he leaned forward to take off his shirt.

Outside, rain was still falling hard. Holly could see Will's bare chest and shoulders in the mirror, and he caught her looking at his reflection. "Come here," he said. He reached behind him for her hands and pulled her arms around his chest; in the mirror she watched him slowly move her hands lower.

"I think you should go home," Holly said again, but she knew he wasn't listening; she was hardly listening, herself. The sound of the rain on the flat roof, and she and Will watching themselves in the mirror—even the dinginess of the motel room had started to affect her. It was a place neither she nor Will was likely to be, and it made Holly feel less responsible, as if they were cut loose from themselves, and this night cut loose from ordinary time. With Will watching, she unbuttoned her blouse and dropped it on the floor; she pulled off her jeans. She took off her bra and let Will take off her panties.

Holly lay back on the bed, with Will over her, his own clothes off; the bedspread under her was green polyester—a bedspread you could do anything on, Holly thought, and no one would see, hear, or ever know.

"Tell me what you want," Will said urgently, "things we've never done, whatever you can think of."

Outside it was thundering. Holly moved her hands up Will's smooth back and then pressed her arms back against the bed, her hands on either side of her pillow. "Hold my wrists like this," she whispered. She closed her eyes and felt the pressure of his hands on hers and the feel of his mouth against her neck. She could hear his hard breathing. "Don't stop," she whispered. He tightened his hold on her. They didn't kiss.

*A*fterward they fell asleep naked on the bedspread, but Holly awoke two hours later. She got up, put on her blouse, and sat in a chair by the window. The air conditioner in the room had come on, and the storm was over. She heard the hissing sound of trucks and cars on the wet highway. She felt wide awake and thought about waking up Will and saying, "Make love to me again," because she was restless and overexcited.

Outside, the parking lot was shiny with water. The light was on in the shabby motel office; the two cars at the motel besides Will's and Holly's were old and beat-up. Holly got a picture in her mind, then, of Will's house, with its chemically treated lawn and edged driveway, his children asleep in their rooms, and her restlessness began to disappear, replaced by an emptiness that increased when she looked at the mirror, the ugly bedspread, the dirty-looking wallpaper.

"Come back to bed," Will said, half-asleep.

Holly lay down next to him. She slept and dreamed that she and Will were naked in her car, driving but not moving, somehow. It was raining in the backseat but not the front, and Evelyn's complaining voice was on the radio.

*T*he motel room was worse in the sunlight. Holly watched a cockroach crawl across the floor from the bathroom to the closet, and before Will was out of the shower she was leaving, shouting to him that she was going home; if he came over, she'd cook him breakfast.

The day was almost cool. Holly drove home with the windows open, past the old drive-in and through Venus, where everyone she saw was in church clothes. On the corner of Venus and Elm, Holly saw Franklin Sanders standing on the steps of the Methodist church, greeting parishioners.

As a child Holly had gone to the Presbyterian church, on Oak. Her mother had taken her. Her father had stayed home Sunday mornings. Church, for Holly, had meant getting a new dress for Easter, attending Sunday school, and meeting her father afterward for Sunday dinner at the Dell Family Restaurant, which had gone out of business twenty years ago. Holly could remember the red dress Gussie and Beatrice's mother would wear and the way it would rustle as she showed Holly and her parents to their table. She was old, in Holly's memory; Holly imagined she'd been sixty or so, younger than either Gussie or Beatrice was now.

Holly drove past the Hearth and the Catholic church, which Will and his family belonged to. When she got home she made coffee and had a picture in her head of a movie she'd seen once, in which a woman killed somebody with an axe and then came home and made breakfast.

"Hi, honey, I'm home," Will joked as he walked into the house. Then he stood in the middle of her living room for a second with his arms in an odd position, because, Holly realized, he'd been in the act of reaching out for her when she'd stepped back.

Holly patted his stomach and went into the kitchen. "All I have for breakfast is oatmeal," she told him over her shoulder.

"Oatmeal's fine."

Will poured himself coffee, and they had breakfast looking out at Holly's yard, which was strewn with leaves and branches from the storm. They didn't talk about anything important, and Holly felt they were behaving like two people who'd met in a bar the night before. Although she didn't really know what that would be like. She'd never done it, though she'd tried once, right after her divorce from Burke. She and Marvelle had been drinking Southern Comfort Manhattans at the Ferrisville Tap on a snowy December night, and Marvelle had prevented her from leaving with a minister named Rowdy Phelps. "If he's a minister, I'm a kangaroo," Marvelle had said later.

Holly told Will that story now, over breakfast. "That's the kind of thing you do when you first leave someone," she told him. "You're all mixed up. You think you understand what you're doing a lot better than you do."

"You're not exactly a stranger to me," Will said.

"I know that," Holly told him. "I'm a good friend."

"Yes, you are. I'd be the envy of every man I know if I had more friends like you." He got up and put his dishes in the sink.

"I didn't mean it that way," Holly started to explain, but Will was already on his way out the door, to open the Hearth. Holly was scheduled to work at eleven o'clock. The only thing they'd agreed on was to still—today at the restaurant, anyway—keep the situation a secret. That was Holly's idea. "I can't serve food while people are picturing us in bed," she'd told Will.

*H*er first thought, however, once she was alone, was to call Marvelle and tell her everything, and she had to talk herself out of it. Marvelle had enough worries of her own. Curtis had started spending all of his free time in the garage, messing with Morgan's motorcycle. "I wake up in the morning thinking it's Morgan out there," Marvelle had told Holly the day before, driving back from the hospital. "One night I got up and made sure none of the guns were loaded." Holly hadn't known how to reassure her. She was worried enough about her own son, and Curtis was a lot more unpredictable and strange than Owen.

Holly got ready for work. She took her uniform out of the dryer; when she saw that the grease stain was still there, she thought, This is going to make Evelyn mad if she sees it. It took her a second to realize that if Will didn't go back home, Evelyn wouldn't have anything to do with the restaurant anymore. Everything would be different. Will might even fire Sue-Ellis, which meant that Sue-Ellis would blame Holly, and that Gene Rollison might not come in as often—not that it mattered, Holly thought, if he was still going to waste his time with Sue-Ellis.

Holly felt shaken. She had never experienced an earthquake—she'd never even set foot in California—but she thought she could imagine how people felt afterward. What she didn't think about until later was that things like affairs, separations, and divorces weren't comparable to natural disasters, unless you thought you were like a china cabinet or a wall—an object things just happened to.

Right then, though, Holly dressed and put on makeup and drove to the Hearth, and as she passed the Presbyterian church she saw the last thing she expected—Curtis, flying out of a side street in his jeep. He sped across Venus Avenue and crashed into a parked car. The accident was over in a second, but for Holly it seemed to happen in slow motion. Even Curtis's surprised expression seemed frozen on his face.

Holly got to the jeep before anyone else. Curtis had been thrown, somehow, into the small backseat. His head was bleeding, and one hand was cut. He looked up at her and said, "Where did that car come from?"

He was drunk. He'd been drinking half the night, he admitted later. There was a broken bottle of Wild Turkey in the jeep—the floor and seat reeked of whiskey.

By the time the paramedics and police arrived, and Marvelle, and Gene Rollison—who'd heard it on his police radio—Curtis had crawled out of the jeep and was sitting on the sidewalk. Holly hadn't been able to stop him. Now he was weeping about Wendy to his mother, saying, "I can't believe she's fucking somebody else."

"It's all right, honey," Marvelle told him. She was kneeling down next to him, tears sliding down her face. A paramedic was trying to clean his head wound.

Will had come running down from the Hearth. He caught up with Holly just as Gene was quickly walking toward her from his police car, looking worried and protective. Holly could see that on his face. She'd taken a step toward him.

"What the hell happened?" Will said. "Are you okay?"

He put his arm around Holly. She looked up to see Gene stop and stand there, watching them.

13

*urtis was all right, for the most part—he'd cracked two
ribs and sprained an ankle and was recuperating at home.
But the news Dick Spearman got from his doctors worsened
each day. Monday all he needed was angioplasty; Tuesday
morning he was told that angioplasty might kill him. Wednesday morning he learned that his major artery was 95 percent
blocked.

" 'It's amazing that your heart attack didn't kill you,' "
Dick said, quoting his doctor. " 'You're lucky to be alive. I'm
scheduling your triple bypass for tomorrow morning.' "

Early Wednesday afternoon, Holly, Marvelle, and Franklin
Sanders drove out to the hospital together to help lift Dick's
spirits.

"Five days ago my biggest problem was having to inseminate too many hogs," Dick told them. "Now I'd give anything to have a hog in front of me. And not on a plate," he said to Marvelle, who hadn't spoken a word yet, who had hardly spoken to Holly and Franklin the whole way to the hospital.

"I wasn't thinking that," Marvelle told him. "I was thinking that what's happening to you is my fault. I don't think I'm safe for men to be around."

"That's ridiculous," Franklin said.

"You two should stay away from me," she told Dick and Franklin. "Really. In fact, I shouldn't be here now. When men get around me they don't feel like living anymore, or else their arteries close up."

She walked out of the room, and Holly found her a few minutes later down the hall on a pay phone, talking to Curtis. "Honey, pack your things as soon as you feel better," she was saying. "I'll pay for an apartment. Or maybe I'll move out. I could get a mobile home."

Holly took the phone out of Marvelle's hand. "Don't worry," she told Curtis. "Your mother's all right. She's just upset. Dick Spearman is having an operation tomorrow."

"I don't care who died," Curtis said. "I'm not moving out of this house." He slammed down the phone.

"Curtis said he was sorry to hear about Dick, and that he hopes you're all right," Holly told Marvelle.

"Did he really?" Marvelle said. "See how sweet he can be? That's the side of him people don't see."

They walked back to Dick's room, Holly trying not to look in the other rooms or at a patient walking slowly past in a robe and slippers. She slowed her own pace. If you weren't sick yourself, Holly thought, if you weren't bedridden, the least you could do in a hospital was not speed-walk down the corridors.

"I feel so bad for these people," she told Marvelle. "I feel guilty for being healthy. Of course I could have some terminal disease and not even know it."

"At least you haven't made anyone else sick, the way I have," Marvelle said.

Dick was sitting up in bed, writing his will. "A small one, just in case," he told Holly and Marvelle, when they came in. "There's no reason not to take precautions."

"That's just common sense," Franklin said. "I don't think it represents a lack of faith."

"Why not?" Marvelle asked him.

"Don't try to back me into a corner about God," Franklin told her. "I know what you're up to."

"All I did was ask a question."

"A question from you is like a torpedo," Franklin said.

Marvelle didn't respond, and in the silence that followed they could hear Dick's mother and Lawson, who'd taken her to lunch in the cafeteria, coming down the hallway. "I've asked God to take me instead," Dick's mother announced. "I've told Him I'm ready to go at a moment's notice."

"Nobody's going anywhere," Dick said when his mother and Lawson walked in.

"You've always had the best ears," his mother told him.

It was three o'clock. Holly and Marvelle kissed Dick and wished him luck; Franklin shook his hand.

"You'll be fine," he told Dick. "I'll see you the day after tomorrow. I can't tell you how many people I've seen go through this operation, and they've almost all lived." He looked around the room at their serious, surprised faces. "I've been trying to use more humor," he explained.

*T*hey drove back to Venus in Franklin's little orange Toyota, Holly sitting in the backseat, looking at Marvelle's unruly red hair and Franklin's neatly trimmed gray hair. The two of them didn't have a thing in common, Holly thought, yet halfway to Venus, when Franklin turned on the radio and a rebroadcast of an old Gussie Dell program came on, both he and Marvelle said, "Lord save us" at exactly the same time.

They listened to Gussie Dell say, "My little grandson, Norman, got into trouble in Sunday school. They were talking about Jesus coming back to life, and Norman said, 'How come nobody ever sees him at the K mart?' I think that's a good question. Why shouldn't Jesus pop up now and then, like Elvis?"

"Why does she have to belong to my church?" Franklin said. "Why can't she torment the Presbyterians or the Baptists?"

They were just north of Venus; Franklin had driven home a slower, more scenic way, on a road that led back into town near Restwell Drive. "Oh, look," Marvelle said, "we're just a few blocks from the cemetery. Let's stop for a minute."

"You make it sound like a tourist attraction," Franklin said.

"All I was thinking was that you could say a prayer over Morgan's grave," Marvelle told him defensively.

"I mention his name every Sunday in church," Franklin said. "It's too bad you're never there to hear it." But he turned onto Restwell Drive anyway, and parked the car. The three of them walked up the steep bank of grass into the cemetery. Holly felt she could walk through it blindfolded, she'd been there so often, and she noticed the way Marvelle cheered up as soon as she saw a gravestone.

"Look," Marvelle said enthusiastically. "They've just begun a Life Everlasting section."

They walked past the hovering angel and Reese Nyles's brother's grave, and then Morgan's grave was in front of them, with all its blooming flowers. "Well, isn't this something," Franklin said. "Have you thought about charging admission?"

"She could enter it in the Venus Garden Show," Holly told him.

"That's not funny," Marvelle said. She got tearful suddenly, and stooped down to weed around a begonia.

"We're not making fun of you," Franklin said gently. "Not exactly. We're worried about this attachment of yours. We have to let the dead go, Marvelle. They're not here for us anymore."

"You don't know how hard that is," Marvelle told him, standing up. "Maybe it's easier if the person gets sick and dies, or if he's in an accident, or if lightning strikes him. But it's different when somebody kills himself. He won't let go of you," she said. "Morgan won't let go of me."

"It just feels that way," Franklin told her, handing her his handkerchief, and right there, in the middle of the cemetery, he put his arms around her.

"I guess I'll just take a little walk," Holly said.

The warm afternoon was breezy. Off in the distance Holly could see white sheets on Sue-Ellis's clothesline puffed up like sails. Farther in the distance she could see the oak and poplar trees that surrounded the elementary school playground. She walked to her father's grave and read the inscription, though she knew it by heart. It didn't affect her much anymore. She almost wished it did, because all at once she felt homesick for some kind of emotion, some strong feeling that would make her want something too much, or at least let her know what she didn't have.

She walked back toward Franklin and Marvelle as they stepped away from each other; Marvelle handed Franklin his handkerchief. By the time Holly reached them, they were laughing a little.

"It's a beautiful day, isn't it?" Franklin said once they got to his car. "I can't remember a day this pretty in years."

*T*hey dropped Holly off at the Hearth. She was scheduled to work that evening; she didn't need her car because Will was going to drive her home afterward and spend the night.

"I can't wait until later," he told Holly, in front of Cleveland, when she walked into the kitchen.

"Don't," Holly said.

"I didn't hear a thing and I don't want to know anything," Cleveland said to both of them.

Holly changed into her uniform and set the tables in the dining room—with Sue-Ellis, when Sue-Ellis finally came in. "I was shopping in Ferrisville and lost track of time," she told

Holly. "I decided you probably have to get out of Kansas to find anything sexy."

"Try a Frederick's of Hollywood catalogue," Holly told her.

"I didn't mean sexy as in tasteless," Sue-Ellis said. She picked up the silverware tray and moved to the opposite side of the room.

The special tonight was chicken and noodles—Owen's favorite; Holly had talked to him that morning, suggesting he come in for dinner, but he'd said no, Crystal was making him spaghetti squash. "It's this cool, yellow, stringy stuff," he'd told Holly, "and she's also making some avocado thing. How do you cook an avocado?"

She finished setting tables and stood at the front counter, looking out at the street, busy with people driving home from work. Customers began coming in at five. A highway crew from Wichita, resurfacing Route 86, occupied two big tables, and soon after that Will's wife walked in with the children and sat in Sue-Ellis's section.

"How are you all?" Holly heard Sue-Ellis say. "I never see you anymore. Doesn't your dad let you out of the house?"

"Dad isn't at our house," the oldest child said.

Sue-Ellis looked up at Holly in what seemed to Holly a suspicious way. "I didn't know that," Sue-Ellis said. "Sometimes it doesn't pay to be a cousin. Sometimes relatives are the last to know anything."

"I like to keep my life private, but you can see how hard that is with little ones," Evelyn said.

Will walked in then and hugged the children. "What a surprise," he said. "I was missing all of you. I was just thinking how much I wanted to see you."

Holly went into the kitchen. She got herself coffee and waited for the highway workers' orders to come up. "I hear children out there," Cleveland said. "Will's?" Holly nodded. "I thought so," Cleveland said. "Don't tell me anything, because I don't want to know, but I don't like to see you people screwing up your lives. It bothers me."

"How can you be happy if you don't change the things that make you unhappy?" Holly said.

"Up here," Cleveland told her, pointing to his head. "You rearrange your thinking."

Sue-Ellis had just come into the kitchen with Evelyn and the children's orders. "I'd like to rearrange Will's head right now," she said.

Holly piled the highway workers' dinners on a big tray and took them into the dining room. The men asked her for extra gravy, ketchup, Cokes with less ice, and, finally, three hours in a motel room with her and Sue-Ellis—though they backed off from Sue-Ellis when Gene Rollison came in, wearing his uniform, and Sue-Ellis put her arm around his waist. He waved to Holly. It gave her a sudden headache, seeing him and Sue-Ellis like that, but she still couldn't make herself avoid him. When she walked past his table he said, "My sister was visiting and brought me bedding plants. I thought you might want them for your garden."

"I'd have to dig up more of my yard first."

"That's the part of gardening I can help you with," Gene told her.

Evelyn and Will had disappeared. They were in the laundry room, it turned out. In the kitchen, later, even through the closed door, Holly could hear them arguing. "I never said

I wanted you to leave," she heard Evelyn say. "You never listen to me. You make things up."

"I can't work under these conditions," Cleveland told Holly as she dished up desserts.

"Do you think I like it?" Holly said. "How do you think it makes me feel?"

"Don't tell me a thing," Cleveland said. "I don't want to know any details."

Holly went into the dining room and delivered plates of pie and bowls of ice cream. A big highway worker with a bushy beard tried to get her to sit on his lap. "Meet me at the Venus Motel later," he said. "Bring a couple of good-looking friends."

"I only have ugly friends, and I'd never set foot in the Venus Motel," she told him.

Across the room, Holly saw Will and Evelyn's youngest child pouring juice on the floor. The two middle children were ripping open sugar packets. And Sue-Ellis, who was supposed to be watching them, was sitting next to Gene, licking blueberry filling off his fork.

*T*he restaurant finally emptied out, except for Will's children, who were occupied with their desserts. Holly and Sue-Ellis bussed tables. "I feel like this night is never going to end," Sue-Ellis said. "I bet you feel that way even more than I do." When Holly didn't look up, Sue-Ellis said, "And poor Gene, in the middle of all this mess, just wanting to have his dinner."

"How was your date with him?" Holly asked.

"Good," Sue-Ellis said. "He has a very healthy appetite."

Holly collected the dirty tablecloths and threw them in a pile on a window table. She felt bad enough about Evelyn, and being here in the room with the children was even worse—this was the first time they'd seemed real to Holly, as people, instead of just facts about Will's life. But worst of all was having to hear about the size of Gene's appetite from Sue-Ellis. Even though she'd asked.

Sue-Ellis walked up and stood next to Holly. "Isn't that Curtis across the street at the gas station?" she asked. Holly looked out the window and saw Curtis's van parked next to the air hose.

"I think he's cute," Sue-Ellis said, "or would be with a perm and some tight jeans."

"The two of you should go out sometime," Holly told her. "You're not that much older than he is. I think you'd like each other."

"Oh, no," Sue-Ellis said. "I have all I can handle right now with Gene."

Will and Evelyn had still not come back into the dining room. Holly went into the kitchen, changed clothes in the rest room, and told Cleveland to tell Will that she was leaving early and would walk home.

She left through the back door and walked down the alley to Venus Park, then down Hawthorne. She lived three miles from the Hearth—less if she cut through people's yards, but she didn't want to run into dogs and fences. By the time she was on Poplar Avenue the sky was dark and the moon had come up—a white sliver Holly could see just above the trees. She found herself wishing for two things: that Sue-Ellis and Curtis Holman would start dating; and that Will, tonight, would get into his car and follow Evelyn and the children home. But when Holly's own house came into view—the porch light on, suddenly reminding her of summer nights she'd played outside until her mother called her in—she saw that Will's car was parked in front. He'd used the house key she'd given him.

"I don't blame you," he said, from the couch, when she opened the door. "I would have run out, too, if I could have. I did, in a way. I asked Sue-Ellis to close up." He was lying down, drinking a beer. "I didn't expect Evelyn to come in tonight," he said. "I'm sorry."

"I didn't hear anything, and I don't want to know anything," Holly said.

"Then could you get me another beer, Cleveland?" Will asked.

Holly went into the kitchen. Will had filled her refrigerator with fruit, bread, and lunch meats he liked, and bottles of Budweiser. "Are you planning to eat all night?" she asked when she came back into the living room.

"Don't be sarcastic. It will take me a little time to find an apartment, that's all. I don't want to be an imposition meanwhile."

Holly had gotten herself a beer, too. She finished her first one and got herself a second, and in the course of the evening she and Will each had four more.

"I should drink more often," Holly said at one point. "After all, that's what most people do to have a good time."

"Some people use heroin," Will said. "Have you thought about trying that?"

"Don't make fun of me."

Holly was sitting on the floor with her back against the couch, and Will slid down next to her. "I'm sorry," he said. "I really am. I know this is hard on you, all my problems being dumped in your lap. I don't know how I'd get through this alone. I don't know what I'd do now if I didn't have you."

"Really?" Holly said. She thought he was almost crying, though it was hard for her to tell. She was too drunk to see his face clearly. "Do you want to see me dance the way Sue-Ellis used to?"

"Right now?" he said, and then, "Sure," when Holly stood up and pulled off her shirt.

"Stay where you are," she told him. She brought out her radio and turned it on; she went into her bedroom and came out wearing not the little outfit Burke had gotten her—she'd cut that up years ago to use as rags—but high heels and a pair of black thong bikini panties Will had given her that night in Tulsa.

"I feel better already," Will said.

Holly danced from the living room into the kitchen and then, in a moment of daring, out the back door, across the yard, and into the branches of her pecan tree, where Will caught up with her. He slid her panties down with one hand. "Leave the shoes on," he whispered.

Holly knelt down and unzipped his pants; she pulled down his boxer shorts—silk ones she'd bought him herself—and felt his hands on the back of her hair, pressing her to him.

Leaves were brushing against her bare shoulders and back, her black panties tangled around her ankles.

From inside the house she could hear, even over her own breathing and Will's, seventies music playing on the radio— "Love the one you're with . . ."—and then she was on the ground, grass in her hair and in Will's, and she had her legs wrapped around him, her high heels leaving, it turned out, sharp little marks on the backs of his thighs.

In bed, later, Holly woke up, still a little drunk, dizzy, forgetting for a second who she was in bed with, even though Will was the only person who'd ever been in that bed with her. She listened to her bathroom faucet dripping and to another noise she didn't recognize, which sounded like static on the radio, but her radio wasn't in the room and it wasn't turned on.

The sound was Will snoring, Holly realized—breathing through his mouth into her ear, and she turned over and faced the other direction.

14

ick Spearman was a good patient. That was what a nurse said about him Saturday afternoon, a week and a half later. But it seemed to Holly that Dick was more depressed each time she and Marvelle saw him. He'd had his bypass surgery and then he'd had a complication, but he was all right now; his doctor had wanted to release him two days ago. His mother had already gone home to Sioux City, and Dick was due to leave the hospital in the morning, to recuperate at Lawson's house.

"I don't feel ready," Dick said. "Why should I? I could have another heart attack and end up right back here, or die on the spot, just like that."

"Or we could kill you," Marvelle said. "That's looking like a possibility."

Holly put the flowers she'd brought Dick into a vase the nurses had given her. It was August, and every day was hot and windy. Holly watered her flowers each morning, and they still looked droopy, including the ones she'd picked for Dick and the fresher ones Gene Rollison had brought her a week ago. He'd used her shovel to dig up a patch of ground at the southern edge of her garden. Sue-Ellis had driven up as he was digging. She'd sat on the porch with Holly, in a halter top and shorts, brightening up when Gene took off his shirt to work in just his jeans and boots. "It's getting hotter out here by the minute," Sue-Ellis had said loudly.

"I don't think so," Gene said, looking up. "I think it's cooled off some."

"He's quick in some ways," Sue-Ellis had whispered to Holly, "but in other ways he's a few blocks behind."

He might seem foolish sometimes, Holly wanted to say, but he's ten times smarter than you—in fact he's smarter and nicer than anyone I know—but instead she'd looked at Gene's broad shoulders and suntanned arms until he noticed her looking. Then he'd looked directly at her, his face both quizzical and challenging, and she'd quickly looked down at the flowers. Three days later she found packages of flower seeds in her mailbox. "In case you'd rather grow them yourself," Gene had written in a note.

At the hospital now, Holly sat in an orange chair, holding the Scrabble game Marvelle had brought; she watched Dick's face as Marvelle listed all the reasons he should be more cheerful. "Number four," Marvelle said. "I've seen your mail when Lawson brings it in, and I've noticed the number of get-well cards you get. People really like you."

"That must be hard for you to believe," Dick said.

"I never disliked you," Marvelle told him. "I just found you irritating."

"Is that reason number five?" Dick asked.

"No," Marvelle said. "That's not on the list."

Reasons five, six, and seven seemed weak to Holly—especially seven, which was that Marvelle's dog, Hoyt, had taken to Dick right away, whereas Hoyt seemed to hate Lawson.

"Find me a dog that doesn't hate a veterinarian," Dick said, and Holly had to agree with that.

And after reason number seven, Marvelle seemed at a loss to continue. She looked down at her hands and picked at a hangnail. For a few minutes the only sound in the room was the air vent, which made clicking noises whenever the hospital air conditioning came on.

"All right," Dick said finally. "Here's number eight. I don't feel so bad anymore about hating my ex-wife. It was something Franklin Sanders said."

"Watch out for him—he'll try to get you into church," Marvelle told him.

"It wasn't about religion, exactly," Dick said. "He told me that he didn't love his wife. He said it plainly as that, and he said that he didn't think it was a sin. He said that he was rethinking sin. You had to separate what you did from what you felt, he said, and then separate what you felt from what you couldn't help feeling."

"Then what were you supposed to do?" Marvelle asked.

"Forgive yourself."

Marvelle was quiet. "I don't think it's as simple as that," she said then. "I don't think you should have to forgive yourself for your feelings."

"But they're not sins God has to forgive," Dick said. "That's the good part."

"The good part would be if you acted on them," Marvelle said. She got up and stood at the window.

Outside, clouds were forming the way they did every hot afternoon—tall cumulus clouds that billowed up in layers. To Holly they seemed to form themselves out of nothing. They were like thoughts that came into your mind when you thought you weren't thinking, which was never, Holly knew; Crystal Turner said you had to practice meditation for years before you could empty your mind, and even then you thought about breathing.

"I don't know," Dick said. "I don't think I should act on mine. I don't think it would be good, what I'd like to do to my ex-wife. You and I must be talking about different kinds of feelings."

Holly pulled her chair close to the bed and set up the Scrabble game. "Sit down," she told Marvelle. "Let's play. We'll let the patient go first."

"I'm a bad speller," Dick said. "I wouldn't bother playing with me if I were you."

"Just make any word you can," Marvelle told him.

"Women are better spellers than men," Dick said. "You don't know how badly I did in high school. I didn't even play sports."

"So you were a loser," Marvelle said. "So what?"

"You don't know the half of it," Dick said. "I can see all the wrong turns I've taken and all the mistakes I've made. That's all there is to do in a hospital. That's why I've been thinking about how I feel. You lie in bed and think about all the problems you have, and all the things you wish you'd done differently."

"You could be reading your *Healthy Heart* book," Marvelle told him.

"That's another thing," Dick said. "All the hours I've spent watching television when I could have been reading books."

A nurse came in and gave Dick a pill to take with his dinner. It was almost five o'clock. From where Holly was sitting she could see Pink Ladies wheeling dinner trays down the white-tiled hall; she could see a man in the room across the hall, sitting alone at the end of his bed. She felt suddenly and selfishly homesick for her own house, for the familiarity of her furniture, for the meals she made in her own kitchen.

"Dick," she said, "don't you want to get out of here? Don't you want your life back?"

He put down the water glass he'd been holding and looked at the blank Scrabble board. "I guess so," he said, "when you put it that way. I guess I do."

𝓑ack in Venus, an hour later, on their way to take Nedra Holman out for dinner—Holly had promised to go with Marvelle and her mother-in-law—they stopped at the Acres of Trailers Park so that Holly could drop off Burke's mail. She suspected that he gave out her address to anyone he owed money to, since the mail that came for him at her house consisted only of bills and overdue notices.

"I'm going to start throwing these in the trash," she told him as she got out of Marvelle's pickup. "I don't know why I haven't already." Burke was sitting outside his trailer in a lawn chair, reading a *Tattoo Art* magazine.

"I'll straighten it out tomorrow," Burke said.

"Your idea of tomorrow is always a few years off." Holly dumped the letters in his lap. Inside, Annette, still wearing her K mart smock, waved to Holly through the screen door.

Holly got back in Marvelle's pickup; they wound their way out of the trailer park on the rutted dirt road. Holly was thinking about how, when she was in high school and wouldn't do her homework, her mother would say, "Do you want to end up working at K mart and living in the Acres of Trailers Park?" Her mother had cried at her wedding—not from happiness—but after a while she and Holly's father had almost started to like Burke; Burke had a careless way about him that looked more easygoing than it was. When Holly first decided to divorce him, her mother thought she should reconsider, but that was before Burke took up with Annette, who had still been in high school.

"Age-wise, Owen and Crystal are just like Burke and Annette, only in reverse," Holly said to Marvelle.

"Boys always want to be like their fathers," Marvelle said, and Holly could tell she was thinking and worrying about Curtis. His injuries were healing, Marvelle had told Holly, but he was brooding over his job, which he'd lost; and his DWI, which he blamed on Wendy Dell; and Wendy Dell, who hung up whenever he called.

They were on Lone Hill Road, and Marvelle pulled into the entrance of the Springhaven Retirement Center. It was still bright outside, the sun low over the cornfields across the road. Holly and Marvelle found Nedra on the small patio out front, dressed in a yellow pantsuit. Her hair was curled, and she'd rouged her cheeks.

"Let's take pictures first," Nedra said.

"I don't have a camera, Nedra," Marvelle told her. "I'm sorry. I don't even own one."

"Not even one of those little ones?" Nedra asked.

"I'm afraid not," Marvelle said.

She and Holly helped Nedra across the uneven flagstones out to the truck. Nedra sat in the middle and told them that a seagull had flown through the dining room during breakfast.

"Right over the scrambled eggs and bacon," Nedra said. "It was a sight. Then it flew right out to sea."

"What sea?" Holly asked.

"The Atlantic Ocean," Nedra said.

They were coming into the outskirts of Ferrisville. Nedra sat up straighter when she noticed the Denny's parking lot Marvelle was pulling into. "I thought we were going to McDonald's," she told Marvelle. "That's what you told me. I had my heart set on it."

"I didn't tell you that—I wanted to treat you to a real dinner," Marvelle said.

"Don't make promises to people if you can't keep them," Nedra said. "That's what my father used to say."

Marvelle turned the truck around and drove across the highway to McDonald's.

"This doesn't look like a McDonald's to me," Nedra said as Holly helped her out of the truck. "Where are we? Where's the beach?"

"Nedra, what place are you thinking of?" Marvelle asked as she opened the door for her. "Are you thinking of a trip you and Vernard took once?"

"We went to Cape Cod on our honeymoon," Nedra said. "That must be what you mean."

"I was trying to find out what you meant," Marvelle said. She left Nedra at a booth with Holly and went up to the counter to order for the three of them.

"I hoped Morgan would be here," Nedra said. "I thought he might surprise me."

She looked across the aisle at a woman with three small children. "That boy in the blue shirt has Morgan's sad face," Nedra said thoughtfully. She put her hands on the table in front of her, and Holly looked at the gold wedding band on her thin, knobby finger.

"That's a pretty ring," she told Nedra.

"It was a present from a friend," Nedra said.

Marvelle brought over their food. Nedra took a bite of her own hamburger and then a bite of Marvelle's, which made Holly understand something about the way Nedra's mind worked—she'd lost track of where things belonged. Her mind was like clothes tumbling in a dryer, Holly thought, with the important things still somehow ending up on top, clinging to a miscellaneous item in the present. Right now, for instance, when Holly finished eating and was putting on lip gloss, Nedra referred to Holly as her sister—dead now some twenty-five years.

"You always thought you were prettier than me," Nedra said. "Don't think I don't know that. Who do you think you're kidding?" She patted Holly's hand. "Never mind. You're still my sister, and I love you anyway."

Marvelle and Holly waited for Nedra to finish her coffee, then they helped her into the truck and drove back to Venus. "I thought we'd drive through town a little," Marvelle said, "just to have an outing."

"Good—I don't get out much," Nedra said.

The sun had set; dusk made the trees looked thicker and darker, the sidewalks pale beneath them. Children were still outside, playing in the small front yards along Elm Street. The streetlights came on. Nedra, next to the window now, mentioned the seagull again, only this time she seemed to be standing on a pier, watching someone catch a fish.

"Morgan was there with me," she said. They were stopped at a red flashing light in front of Venus Elementary School. "He must have been nine or ten. The school principal was right next to him, eating a hot dog."

"What was Morgan doing?" Marvelle asked Nedra. "Can you remember exactly?"

"Oh, honey," Nedra said. "You know Morgan. He was picking up dead birds and throwing them right into the ocean."

They drove past Venus Fabrics, where Nedra had once worked, and past the church she'd attended, and finally past the small, brown house on Gentilly Street where Nedra and her husband had lived for thirty-eight years. A light was on in the upstairs window.

"I used to know the people who lived there," Nedra said.

It was dark by the time Holly and Marvelle took her back to Springhaven. They walked her to her room and, in the yellow glow from the nightlight, helped her change into her nightgown. Her tiny-boned roommate, Estelle Henry, was in bed, asleep, breathing noisily.

"Hush up, Mrs. Henry," Nedra said.

Then she got into her own bed, which was next to the window, and in the dimly lit room Holly and Marvelle could see her bright eyes, wide open.

*A*fterward, Marvelle suggested a change of scenery and a drink. They turned around and drove to the Best Western, off the interstate in Ferrisville. Thursdays through Saturdays there was live music in the Silver Spur Lounge; Holly and Marvelle sat in a booth and watched the country-and-western band set up their equipment. They were the only customers so far except for a man in a business suit sitting at the bar.

A waitress came over to take Holly and Marvelle's order— Jenny Dyer, Holly realized, in a short red dress, black panty hose, and high heels. Holly said hello to her by name.

"Do we know each other?" Jenny asked.

"We were in an aerobics class together," Holly said helpfully.

"Were we?" Jenny pushed back her long hair and smiled at Holly. "I've been in so many of those."

Before long, the lights were turned down and the band began to play. Cars were pulling into the parking lot, their headlights shining briefly through the window. Soon the room was noisy and smoky and the dance floor was crowded. Holly and Marvelle took turns dancing with a small man in a cowboy hat, from Oklahoma. During slow songs with Marvelle, he nestled his head under her neck, reminding Holly of the sweet way she'd once seen tropical birds sleep. She herself was only dancing with him to the fast songs, because during a slow dance he'd helped himself to a kiss.

At eleven-thirty, while the Oklahoma man was up at the bar buying drinks, Reese Nyles came in by himself, in a white shirt and new jeans, his hair pulled back in a small ponytail.

"Reese!" Holly called out to him. She slid over and he sat beside her. "I bet you already know this, but Jenny Dyer's working here," she told him.

"I know. That's why I came." He looked eagerly around the crowded room. "She didn't expect to end up working in a bar," he told Holly and Marvelle, "so I'm hoping she's ready to change her mind and give me another chance. Sometimes people don't see what's right in front of them."

"I don't think that's going to happen," Marvelle said. She pointed to a table across the room where Jenny was kissing a customer.

Reese looked at Jenny, got up, and left without speaking.

"Did you have to do that?" Holly said to Marvelle. She watched the door close behind him. "I'll be right back."

Out in the parking lot, she found Reese leaning against his old car. She could faintly hear the band playing.

"Stop choosing women who leave you," Holly said. "Sometimes I think you want to be lonely."

"Of course I don't," Reese told her. "Why would anybody want that?"

But the look on his face reminded Holly of his expression, years ago, the afternoon she'd run into him at the cemetery; now she suddenly understood why she'd imagined, or hoped, that day, that there was something between them. He was so removed all the time—untouchable, almost, like the pope, or like God, Holly thought, so that if you felt just a little closer to him, you felt as if you mattered more, as if your own life were more important.

"Do you think you really love Jenny?" Holly asked. "I mean, love is complicated. It's not like it's easy to know how you feel."

Reese took off his glasses and rubbed his eyes. He looked as solitary as anyone Holly had ever seen.

"I love her as much as I can love anybody," he said.

Holly and Marvelle didn't leave until the Silver Spur closed. Then they stopped at an all-night donut shop and drove home on Ferrisville Road, past Gene Rollison's trailer. His car wasn't there. Holly put down the donut she was eating and asked Marvelle for a sip of coffee; her throat was suddenly tight and dry.

"Was his car there?" Marvelle asked.

"Whose car?" Holly said.

"Whose do you think?"

"No," Holly said, feeling caught. "At least I didn't see it. Of course I didn't look that closely." She turned her head away from Marvelle, toward her own nervous reflection in the side window.

"That might not mean anything," Marvelle told her "Sometimes he works all weekend. I wouldn't worry about it."

"Why would I worry about it?" Holly said.

"Why did you look, then?" Marvelle asked.

"I just glanced over. I didn't look on purpose."

"I guess his trailer just happened to be in the spot you looked at," Marvelle said.

"It's a mobile home, not a trailer," Holly told her. "Trailers are what people like Burke live in." Her voice was shaky, and she could feel Marvelle's eyes on her. "Watch the road," she said. "Don't look at me like I'm crazy."

"Then don't act crazy," Marvelle said. "Tell the truth." Holly opened her window and cleared her throat. After a few minutes Marvelle said, "Why do small men always want to go home with me? It's like they're mountain climbers, and I'm the peak."

"Gene Rollison isn't small."

Marvelle slowed down and looked at Holly. "Gene is history for me, and vice versa," she said, "and he was my idea more than I was his. I've told you that."

"Now he's Sue-Ellis's," Holly said. She put her head back against the seat. She couldn't talk to Marvelle about Gene and didn't know what to say anyway. Even if you knew how you felt, she thought, why should you trust your feelings in the first place, knowing how much trouble they'd gotten you into in the past?

Holly closed her eyes. She could smell Nedra Holman's too sweet powder in the truck. Nedra's room at the retirement center had smelled of it. Holly imagined it had gotten into her own clothes and hair, along with the smoke from the Silver Spur Lounge. Right now, Holly thought, she and Marvelle smelled like Nedra in a bar. Marvelle said that Nedra used to drink—especially at family get-togethers. She fell over a picnic bench once, and another time she stepped into a bowl of macaroni salad. And Holly could remember Morgan dancing with Nedra at a wedding reception—the two of them almost flying into the table that held the punch bowl. It was so long ago that Holly couldn't remember whose wedding it was.

"Does Nedra ever drink anymore?" she asked Marvelle.

"She can't," Marvelle said. "She gets even more confused and then cries."

They were driving into Venus, with its empty streets and dark houses. Holly had left her own lights on: the porch light and the lights in her living room. Will was spending the night with his children—Evelyn had gone to Kansas City to see her parents.

Marvelle pulled up in front of Holly's house, and Holly said good night. She walked past her mimosa tree, past the flowers Gene had given her, and up her brightly lit steps.

15

ill Chaffe moved into an apartment the second week of
August. It was on the first floor of a new complex on
Walnut Avenue, across from Luciano's Pizza. At first he didn't
have any furniture and spent the nights at Holly's house, but
then his oldest child, Toddy, started calling him at work in the
morning. "Where were you last night, Dad?" he'd say. "I
wanted to tell you something." Will went out and bought a
mattress, a couch, and a kitchen table.

His relationship with Holly wasn't a secret anymore, although nobody seemed surprised. Marvelle said she'd suspected it for a while, ever since she noticed Will giving Holly
the pickle off his hamburger plate. Sue-Ellis wondered aloud
at just how stupid Holly and Will thought their coworkers

were. But Holly kept her distance from Will at work; it made her uncomfortable that people knew, and lately Evelyn had found out as well. She called Holly's house sometimes, asking for Will; she called Will at work with news about the children—conversations that almost always ended, on both sides, with accusations and shouting.

Even Holly's mother had found out somehow, and sent Holly clippings from Ann Landers, letters written by "Sadder But Wiser" or "The Other Woman." Her mother's point was that if Will could cheat on his wife, why couldn't he cheat on Holly? Holly hadn't expected so many people to think that it was easy for a man to leave his wife and children. Will felt guilty all the time, and by the end of August he had lost fifteen pounds. And he'd been thin to start with.

"You need to eat foods that are fattening," Holly told him in the kitchen at the Hearth early on a Saturday evening. The only customer so far was Curtis Holman, whom Sue-Ellis was waiting on; they'd discovered a common interest in dressing deer.

"You know what I feel like eating?" Will said to Cleveland. "One of those sandwiches you used to make for Evelyn."

"Why?" Cleveland asked him.

"I don't know why," Will said. "Who cares? It's what I'm in the mood for."

The phone rang then; it was Will's six-year-old daughter, telling him she'd just lost a tooth. Will had tears in his eyes by the time he hung up. Holly brought him a Kleenex and went out into the dining room and sat down across from Curtis.

"What?" Curtis said, his coveralls greasy, his dark blond hair loose around his face.

"Nothing. I just wanted some company." Sue-Ellis was standing there, holding a coffeepot. "Can you pour me some?" Holly asked.

"Only if you're a paying customer," Sue-Ellis told her, but she poured her a cup anyway.

"What's your mother doing tonight?" Holly asked Curtis.

"Grooming Hoyt," Curtis said.

"She has an unnatural interest in that dog," Sue-Ellis said. Holly gave her a critical look. "Well, she does. Everybody around here seems to be interested in the wrong thing lately."

"Why are you so judgmental?" Holly said. "You and your three ex-husbands."

"I thought it was two," Curtis said.

"It is two," Sue-Ellis told him.

"Am I the only adult in Venus who's never been married?" Curtis asked, depressed.

"Yes," Holly and Sue-Ellis both said.

Holly went back into the kitchen, where Will and Cleveland were sitting at the table. Evelyn's favorite sandwich was in front of Will, untouched.

"I can't stop thinking about Jeri Lee's tooth," he said when Holly walked in. "It's such a big event when children lose their teeth."

"It's a bigger event when they're teenagers," Cleveland said.

That night after work, Holly and Will sat outside Will's apartment next to the pool the owner hadn't filled yet. It was a warm night. In an apartment on the other side of the pool, someone was having a party. People were walking in and out, holding drinks. The moon was rising behind the trees that separated the apartment complex from the grounds of the Baptist church.

"Reese Nyles came in with a new date tonight," Holly said. "A woman his own age, for a change."

"I hope it works out. Reese deserves to be happy." Will stretched out his legs. He was barefoot, still dressed in the white shirt and dark pants he'd worn at the Hearth. Holly, who'd already undressed and showered, was wearing his brown robe.

"Everybody should be happy," she told him. "Why should one person deserve it more than another?"

"Because Reese never hurt anyone. His wife left him, and Jenny Dyer left him, and Reese is still alone."

"I left Burke," Holly said. "Does that mean I don't deserve to be happy?"

"Why are you trying to start an argument?" Will asked.

"Well, I feel like it, I guess. Or maybe I just don't agree with you. Do you think that might be possible?"

Holly got up and went inside and for a few minutes wandered angrily around Will's apartment. She'd liked it at first—the clean white walls and beige carpeting, but now she felt tempted to move a footstool out of place, if Will had had a footstool, or run a dangerous electric cord right across the middle of the living room.

In Will's bedroom, Holly watched the phone machine flashing red—messages from Evelyn, she imagined, that Will couldn't bring himself to listen to. She couldn't blame him,

really—sometimes Evelyn even put the crying children on—
and it upset Holly, too. It made her feel like a criminal.

"What are you doing in here?" Will asked her. He'd come
in through the bedroom's sliding glass door.

"I'm asleep," Holly said.

"You can't be. You're standing up."

"I'm sleepwalking," Holly told him, and she walked out
into the hall and into the dark living room, empty except for
Will's new couch with its soft cushions.

Will followed her. He stood behind her and put his hands
on her shoulders, sliding off the robe she was wearing and
letting it fall.

"Let's give you a dream," he said.

"Let's not," Holly told him, but he was touching her neck
and shoulders, and she thought: Why not? What difference
did it make? What was she supposed to do—go home and sit
alone, waiting for the phone to ring, or for Gene to come
over with Sue-Ellis, bringing more secondhand flowers?

Will took off his clothes and pulled her down onto the
couch, on top of him, kissing her so hard she felt his teeth
against her upper lip. "I want to look at you," he said in his
low voice; he sat her up and put his hands on her waist and
moved her against him, the room dark and empty around
them.

Holly closed her eyes. She concentrated not on Will but
on how he felt, under her, and how she felt, and soon she
imagined it was Gene beneath her, looking at her breasts; she
imagined that Gene's hands were on her hips and that it was
Gene breathing hard, saying, "Holly" and "Move faster" and

"Come when I do." If she opened her eyes she'd see his green eyes and strong features, his sunburned shoulders, and she could lean down and press herself against his chest. His arms went around her, and she almost said his name. She almost couldn't stop herself.

Then Will became Will again, and Holly disentangled herself, went into the bedroom, and sat in front of the open window. The answering machine was flashing red in the corner; outside were the sounds of voices and music.

"What's wrong?" Will said, coming into the room. "Get into bed with me." He pulled the sheet back and lay down; Holly got in next to him. "Tell me what's wrong," he said again.

"Nothing," she told him. "I'm tired."

"Me too," he said, and then, "I love you." He was asleep within a few minutes.

Holly lay awake, looking at the ceiling. She was starting to hate the word *love*—she hated the way people used it, or blamed you for not using it, or let it be the reason for whatever they chose to do or not to do. Just once, Holly thought, she'd like to hear someone say, "I fell in jealousy," or "I couldn't stop myself because I was in sadness."

Then, suddenly, it wasn't love but herself she hated. She hated herself for the way she felt now. She wanted to go back in time to when she did love Will, or thought she did—the past a safer place, distant enough to seem better than it was; and more hopeful because the outcome hadn't happened yet. Now she understood why, after Morgan died, Marvelle had kept her up all night, looking at old photographs. Holly remembered one in particular—the light shining on Morgan's face in a way that seemed to capture the person he could or should have been. Marvelle had been in love with that picture.

Things were quieter outside. She heard cars start and drive away.

"What for?" Will muttered in his sleep. "What good will that do?"

The weather was stormy in the morning. It had thundered and rained before daylight, when Holly had woken in Will's arms and thought, I was just tired last night; that's why I was in a bad mood. That's what was wrong with me. I just needed sleep.

She went home at ten, as the sky was darkening again. Owen was sitting on her front steps.

"I lost my key," he said.

"How did you get here? Did Crystal drop you off?"

"I walked from her apartment." Owen followed Holly into the house and got a Coke out of the refrigerator. "Where were you?"

"Running errands," Holly said, even though she was wearing her uniform from the night before.

"Crystal has company," Owen told her. "Some asshole she used to know in Lawrence just showed up this morning out of nowhere, so I told her, 'I'm out of here.' "

"Maybe they're just old friends," Holly said.

"Get real," Owen said.

Holly made breakfast; when it was ready Owen had disappeared from the house. He was outside, in the front yard,
standing next to her flower garden. "You made this bigger,"
he said accusingly. "Why didn't you let me do it?"

"I can't afford you. Gene Rollison did it for nothing. Just
to be helpful."

"Well, he did a shit job," Owen said. "It's not even around
the edges."

They ate breakfast. Crows were flying back and forth
among Lawson's trees. Owen was watching them. "Birds get
restless before a storm," he said, not looking at Holly. "They
can sense things about the weather better than we can."

He drank his juice. He'd let his hair grow a little, which
made his eyes look darker; Holly thought he looked older.
She watched him get up, put his plate on the counter, and
open the back door. The wind caught the screen door and
banged it open against the outside wall.

"Dad cheats on Annette," he said, without turning around.
"A woman calls and hangs up when Annette answers. I an-
swered once and she thought I was Dad." He walked outside.
"It's a shitty thing to do. Annette believes whatever he says."

"She'll probably catch on sooner or later," Holly told him.

"He's the one who should change," Owen said. "He's the
one who's fucking up." He shut the screen door behind him.
"I'm going for a walk," he told Holly.

He crossed the yard, jumped Spring Ditch, and headed out
into the open field. The rain began soon after that. Holly
stood at the kitchen door, hoping he'd come right back;
when he didn't, she went into his bedroom and sat on the
bed. She looked at his posters: a male lead singer wearing

white lipstick, an MTV woman with a pierced tongue, and an old poster of Jimi Hendrix that had once been Burke's. None of them seemed to fit Owen anymore. She wasn't sure what would—he was becoming somebody she liked better but who she couldn't predict anymore. She was afraid for him in a more complicated way than she used to be; she was more worried about what was in his head than what was crashing into it.

He came back an hour later, soaked and cold; he took a shower and put on old clothes he'd left in his closet—jeans and a T-shirt, now both too small for him. He sat in the kitchen with Holly while she made soup out of the leftovers in her refrigerator.

"Some of that stuff has crossed the border into garbage," he told her.

"Throw out what doesn't look good, then," Holly said. "I'm probably thinking too much like Grandma. She used to take things out of the garbage to put into soup."

"You're kidding," Owen said.

"She did once, anyway."

The rain had gotten heavier. Holly could see it pouring out of Lawson's new gutters next door, and then she saw Lawson come out on his steps in a gray poncho. He had his hood up, and he ran from his clinic to her house and knocked on the kitchen door.

"I'm nursing a dog I operated on this morning," he told Holly when she let him in. "She got hit by a car. I don't know if she'll make it or not." He took off his poncho and sat at the table with Owen. "I haven't seen you in a long time," he said. "How's school?"

"I don't know—it starts tomorrow," Owen told him.

"I bet you're not looking forward to that. I know how I felt about school."

"How?" Owen asked.

"Well, you know," Lawson said. "The way everybody does. The way you do, I imagine." He looked up at Holly. "What are you cooking that smells so good?"

"Garbage," Holly told him.

"Soup," Owen said.

"Well, good. There's nothing I like better than soup." Then Lawson stood up suddenly, shook Owen's hand, and put on his poncho. He said good-bye to Holly and ran back through the rain to his clinic.

"I don't remember him being so weird," Owen said.

"He has a crush on me."

"No shit?" Owen said. He turned on Holly's radio, changing the station from country hits to classic rock-and-roll. "Did Crystal call while I was in the shower?" he asked his mother for the second time.

"No," Holly said.

He left the room, and Holly heard the front door open; when she checked on him he was lying on the porch swing with his eyes closed, his legs thrown over one end. Just beyond the overhang, rain was soaking her flowers.

"Did you fall asleep?" she asked him later, when she brought him out a bowl of soup.

"Maybe," he said. "I don't think so." He sat up to eat. "Did anybody call?"

"No."

The rain became drizzle. Owen was looking out at the road as if something were materializing that Holly couldn't see. It was six o'clock. Next door, Lawson had the lights on in his clinic.

Owen put his bowl down on the porch floor. He had shadows under his eyes; his face was creased from the wooden slats of the porch swing. He looked both childlike and adult at the same time. "I wonder if that dog lived," he said to his mother.

16

It rained all the next day and into the evening. Franklin Sanders came into the Hearth by himself for dinner, his wife, he said, being in Topeka at a retreat for ministers' spouses. He was the Hearth's only customer.

"It's been so dreary all day," Marvelle said. She and Holly were sitting with Franklin while he ate catfish. Marvelle was watching him carefully remove the bones.

"Wendy Dell is engaged to the assistant principal at the middle school," she told Franklin. "I just found out this morning. I don't know what Curtis will do when he finds out. I'm not going to tell him. I can't bring myself to."

"You should," Franklin said.

"I can't. I'm afraid. And he'll hate me for it."

"I don't normally think of you as timid," Franklin told her.

"You mean cowardly, right? You think I don't know what you're thinking?"

Marvelle got up and walked to the window and put her hands on the glass, not seeing, as Holly did, Franklin color slightly, and look down at his food. "You know what I think?" Marvelle said, walking back over. "I think Morgan killing himself scared Wendy away from Curtis."

"Wouldn't it scare anybody?" Franklin asked.

"Sometimes I wonder whose side you're on," Marvelle said.

"You know better than that," he told her quietly. They looked at each other, and Holly, suddenly feeling like an intruder, went into the kitchen to put on a pot of coffee.

"Will's in the walk-in cooler," Cleveland told her.

"I wasn't looking for Will," Holly said. "Just because I walk into a room where he might be doesn't mean that's why I walked into it."

Cleveland disappeared into the storeroom, and Holly sat down and watched the coffee drip; when it was done she brought Cleveland a cup, by way of apology.

*T*he next morning she was back at the Hearth again, to work the lunch shift. She stood at the door and watched Gussie Dell crookedly park her silver Lincoln. Wendy was sitting next to Gussie, and Wendy's fiancé was in the backseat. Gussie Dell was famous for her bad driving. A week ago Holly had heard her say on "Neighbor Talk," "What's wrong with parking on the sidewalk? It's concrete, isn't it?"

It was just after eleven. The day was sunny and hot—the first of September. Outside, Gussie was making her way across the street like a small cannon, flanked on one side by Wendy and on the other by Wendy's fiancé.

"The man with the big desk," Marvelle said now, bitterly, coming up behind Holly to watch. She'd been irritable since she came to work, and she'd brought Hoyt to the restaurant, hiding him in the laundry room. "I don't care if Will finds out," she'd told Holly. "Hoyt gets ignored at home. Curtis is always in the garage. I want my dog with me."

Gussie came in wearing a yellow hat with a silk rose pinned on top. "Can you see me from way over there?" she called out to Will as she sat herself and her family at a window table. "The woman who sold me this hat said Jesus would be able to spot me from heaven. I think she was a Baptist."

"I'd say she was right," Will said. He brought the three of them menus.

"I've heard gossip about you," Gussie told him loudly enough for Holly to hear. "Everybody and his sister is criticizing you. Of course you're the only one who knows the real story. I bet you can't wait to set us straight."

"No," Will said, "not really." He walked away, leaving them to Holly, who brought water and coffee and told them about the special—chicken-fried steak with mashed potatoes and gravy.

"That's what I want," Gussie said, "only make it low-calorie."

"I don't think we can do that," Holly told her.

"People are always in a hurry to say that something can't be done," Gussie said. "It's easier to say no than yes. Something follows from yes. Nothing follows from no. Tell Cleveland Harris to use his imagination." Wendy ordered the dieter's plate, and her fiancé ordered a club sandwich and fries.

In the kitchen, Holly relayed Gussie's message.

"I'll give her low-calorie," Cleveland said. Holly watched him broil a round steak and put it on a plate with a baked potato. "Take her this along with a bottle of ketchup," he told Holly. "And tell her she can mash the potato with her fork."

"Are you kidding?"

"It's as imaginative as I get," Cleveland said. "Tell her that, too."

"You go out there and tell her." Holly said.

"My imagination is needed here in the kitchen."

"This isn't what I ordered," Gussie said when Holly served her her lunch. "I'd have to dance on this steak in my high heels before it was tender enough to eat. And why should I have to mash the potato myself? Will Chaffe," she shouted over the noise in the restaurant, "are you taking out your personal problems on your customers?"

"Bring Mother something that looks fattening but isn't," Wendy whispered to Holly.

"Mrs. Dell, would you like to trade lunches with me?" said Wendy's fiancé. "I'd be happy to eat your food."

"I bet you would," Gussie said, "now that you've helped yourself to my daughter." She handed her plate back to Holly. "I wish my sister was here. She always knows what I feel like eating."

Gussie looked at the fiancé's sandwich, and at Wendy's diet plate; then she told Holly she'd settle for the regular lunch special.

Holly and Will brought it out to her together. "If it makes you feel any better," Will told Gussie, "the gravy is made from a low-fat mix."

"Oh, Will," Gussie said. "You advertise home cooking and then serve up mixes?"

$\mathscr{T}$he Hearth was a lot quieter after they left, even during the lunch rush at noon. Holly was hoping that Gene would come in. She had looked up whenever the door opened, then got angry at herself each time. Finally, standing at the window, she saw his state police car; she watched him stop for the light, drive past two available parking spaces, and disappear down Venus Avenue.

Soon after that Evelyn dropped off the two middle children—Jeri Lee and Harrison—whom Will settled at a table near the back. They were six and seven years old.

"What did you do over the summer?" Holly asked when she brought them ice cream sundaes.

"I saw a cat die in the street," Jeri Lee said. Harrison said he didn't do anything.

They both got chocolate sauce on their chins, which Holly would have wiped off except that she felt afraid of these children, as if, if she touched them, they'd turn into monster-sized versions of themselves and take their revenge on her. Looking down at their small heads, however, she felt ashamed of herself. They were just like any children, she thought, preoccupied with sweets and playing, counting on adults to take care of them.

The door opened, and Dick Spearman walked in—thinner, paler, slow-moving, but smiling. Holly hadn't seen him since he left the hospital. Marvelle had visited him four or five times.

"This is my first public appearance," he told them.

Marvelle sat him in the first booth, taking his arm and helping him in. She patted his balding head.

"I'm not Hoyt," he said. He looked at a menu. "I want a hamburger, fries, and a milk shake."

"You're dreaming," Marvelle told him.

"I know. I'll have whatever. I don't care. Decide for me."

Marvelle brought him a glass of decaffeinated iced tea and sat down across from him. "Cleveland's making something special for you. You'll love it."

"Tell me what's been happening," Dick said. "All I hear from Lawson is news about pets."

"Nothing," Marvelle said, "at least nothing good. I never see my son unless I go out to the garage for something, or unless I'm up at three in the morning, when he watches TV. And now his girlfriend is engaged to somebody else."

"Ex-girlfriend, you mean," Dick said.

"All right, ex-girlfriend," Marvelle said. "What difference does it make? How does that change anything?"

"You thought I was a nicer person when I was sick, didn't you?" Dick said. "Didn't she?" he asked Holly, who was sitting at the next table, sponging off plastic menus.

"You did treat him that way," Holly told Marvelle.

Will walked up just then, putting his hand on Holly's shoulder, and Holly got up and put the clean menus on the front counter. Will touching her, with his kids in the room and in front of Dick, made her angry.

"Why are you all ganging up on me?" Marvelle asked. Holly could hear the tears in her voice; a second later Marvelle was out of the booth and walking quickly toward the kitchen.

"I don't know how to talk to her now that I'm not dying," Dick said.

After a while Marvelle came back, more composed, bringing Dick's lunch—a double vegeburger and steamed strips of zucchini. "Don't make that face," she told him. "You won't believe how tasty it is."

"True enough," Dick said.

In the back of the restaurant, Will's children were playing with toy cars Will had bought for them. Jeri Lee had hers on the floor; Harrison had created a race course around the empty sundae dishes, in between the salt and pepper shakers and over the backs of the spoons. Will moved both kids to a clean table and brought them paper and crayons. "Draw cows and pigs for Mr. Spearman," he told them.

Dick was making his way through his vegeburger; Holly had never seen an adult eat so slowly. "Do you know who has the best Polish sausage in the world?" he said to Marvelle, who was watching him eat. "A little diner in Cedar Rapids."

"Hog fat and preservatives," Marvelle said.

Holly reset the next booth and looked out the window at the drooping leaves of a dogwood tree. From the back of the kitchen she could hear Hoyt starting to whine.

"Tell me that's not your dog," Will said to Marvelle.

"I can't," Marvelle told him, hurrying off to the kitchen.

"Will," Dick said, "can you bring me a little meat? A piece of ham or something?"

"Are you kidding? Have you ever seen Marvelle angry?"

Holly stopped setting tables. "You can eat ribs," she told Dick. "You can smoke. You can eat Polish sausage while you're walking in front of a truck. Just don't do any of it in front of Marvelle."

"It was a joke," Dick said. "Sort of."

"Holly and Marvelle are both in bad moods," Will told him.

"We are not," Holly said, and she got up, turned her back on both men, and went over to the kids' table. For a few minutes she watched Jeri Lee draw a picture of a horse, making the tail with the letter *S*, the way Holly herself used to as a child.

"It's a tail," Jeri Lee told her.

"I know it's a tail," Holly said.

Dick Spearman had finished his lunch. He'd shifted in the booth to lean against the wall; his eyes were closed. "I get tired," he told Holly when she cleared away his plate. "Just eating a meal wears me out."

"That's all the more reason to take care of yourself."

"Give me some credit," Dick said. "I'm not so stupid I don't see who my friends are."

*I*n the afternoon, instead of going home at three, as they could have, Holly and Marvelle cleaned out the kitchen cabinets. It was that kind of day, Holly thought, too hot, still, and bright outside at the end of a hot summer—you had to keep busy to stop feeling restless. Even Cleveland, usually home by this time, was experimenting with a recipe for gazpacho, ignoring Will saying, earlier, "No one in this town is going to eat anything with a foreign name, let alone soup that's cold."

The radio was on. It was tuned to the golden oldies station from Topeka. A song Marvelle could remember from high school, Cleveland could remember from junior high, and Holly from grade school. Will was in his office with the door closed, bookkeeping; he never recognized any of the songs anyway. Once, when he didn't recognize "Louie, Louie," Cleveland said, "That's the saddest thing I've ever heard. What was he doing as a kid? Why didn't he have his radio on?"

"Pipeline" was playing. Marvelle was working on the upper cabinets while Holly scrubbed out the ones below. "Look at this present from Sue-Ellis," Holly said. She showed Marvelle three yellow mustard containers filled with ketchup.

"How could anybody do that?" Marvelle asked.

"I'll tell you how," Holly said. "Her mind is on getting Gene Rollison into bed. If it hasn't already happened."

Marvelle rinsed out her wet rag. "Gene is somebody who thinks about what he's doing before he does it," she told Holly. "He doesn't try to take advantage of people. He doesn't—well, you know what I mean."

"I don't think Sue-Ellis is used to that," Holly said.

A few minutes later, when Holly was correcting Sue-Ellis's mistake, the back door opened and Gene walked in. He was off-duty, dressed in jeans and the green shirt that Holly had noticed before. He stood at the far end of the kitchen. Holly couldn't remember anyone other than employees ever using that door before.

"I know you're closed until five," he said awkwardly, "but I saw your cars in back, and wondered if I could just get a cup of coffee."

"Closed means closed," Cleveland said, from behind the stove.

"Of course you can," Marvelle told Gene. "Sit down. I'll make a fresh pot."

Gene walked across the kitchen and sat at the wooden table. He didn't quite look at Holly, who was standing in front of the cabinet with a rag in her hand. He tried to cross his legs and bumped his knee on the edge of the table. Holly, Marvelle, and Cleveland were all watching him.

"I can't drink fast-food coffee," he said finally. "I'm spoiled by the coffee here."

"Maybe you're spoiled by the way Sue-Ellis makes it," Holly said rudely. She ignored the look Marvelle gave her.

"Sue-Ellis makes coffee the way she fills mustard containers," Marvelle told Holly.

"It's not just the coffee," Gene said. He looked down at his hands. Then he looked up at Holly. "I wanted to ask how the flowers were doing," he said.

Marvelle disappeared into the laundry room.

"They're fine," Holly said.

"Are they healthy?" Gene asked.

"Pretty much," Holly told him.

They each looked away in different directions.

"The rain helped," Holly offered then.

"We could still use more," Gene said. He turned his face away from Cleveland, who was standing at the stove with a spoon in his hand, looking at him.

"I like the sound of rain," Gene said quietly. "I like to lie in bed at night, listening to it."

Holly walked over to the coffeemaker. She picked up the pot and filled Gene's cup; she stood next to him longer than she needed to. She looked at his hair, which was beginning to streak with gray, the way hers was. She saw that up close, his green shirt was faded a little, and that his face and neck had been exposed too much to the sun—he was older than she was by just a few years. She turned toward him so that her uniform brushed against his shoulder, even though Cleveland was standing just ten feet away.

"How the hell did we spend fifty dollars on lettuce?" Will said loudly, coming suddenly out of his office.

He saw Gene then, and Holly with the coffeepot.

"Oh," he said. "I didn't know we had a customer." He smiled at Gene and sat down across from him. "Would you pour me some, too, please?" he asked Holly.

He closed the account book he was holding and took the cup Holly handed him. He patted her on the arm.

"You must be high on Holly's list," he told Gene. "Even I don't rate fresh coffee. You should come around here more often."

17

By the time school was in its third week, in the middle of a hot September when only the red tips of the dogwood leaves revealed that fall was coming, Crystal Turner had stopped seeing Owen. She broke up with him gradually at first, seeing him one night but not the next, twice letting him sleep over, and then suddenly she was gone. Holly didn't even see her jogging anymore, though she knew that Crystal was still in Venus, still teaching school. She'd vanished back into her own life, Holly thought, leaving Owen alone with his.

Owen spent more time now with Holly, or in her house, anyway. He had become so quiet Holly would be startled, coming upon him in the living room or on the front porch. He was attending school but not bringing home books. She had expected him to start smoking again, to go out drinking with his friends, to be rude to her—all the things he'd done in the past and that she was prepared for. But now he wasn't so much as skipping school. He'd become just a presence. Sometimes he would almost remind Holly of Hoyt; she spoke nicely to him, she stepped over him, she fed him.

"Honey, you have to talk about your feelings," she told him Wednesday night after dinner, as she wiped off the table. He hadn't said a word since coming home from school, and he'd hardly eaten anything.

"That's bullshit," he said. "I talked to Crystal all the time. So what? I wish I hadn't."

He went out the kitchen door and crossed the backyard. The sun was setting, the cattails along Spring Ditch catching the last of the light. Holly watched Owen jump the ditch and jog into the field on the same path he took the Sunday it rained so hard.

Holly put away the clothes she'd bought for him the day before, still in a shopping bag in his room. He'd outgrown all of his old clothes. Two weeks earlier he'd packed them in boxes, planning to donate them to a halfway house in Ferrisville. Crystal had told him about it.

He'd put the boxes in the trunk of the car Burke had gotten him just before school started—a ten-year-old Honda Civic. Owen hardly used the car except for driving to school and back and forth between Holly's house and Burke's trailer. It was bare and clean inside, except for the boxes in the trunk; Holly imagined they were still there. The car looked as unoccupied as Owen himself had looked lately, his face blank except when Holly happened to see it in an unguarded moment. He'd taken his posters down from his walls, and his portable CD player was unplugged and pushed back neatly into a corner. He'd become neater in general. After he took his shower in the morning, his wet towel, hung up, was the only sign that he'd been in the bathroom.

The nights were growing cooler, but the days, this one especially, were warm for this time of year. Holly sat on the porch, the door open so that she'd be able to hear Owen come back in. The frogs and crickets were as noisy as they'd been in the summer.

Lawson was still next door; his Cherokee was out front, and Holly could see the light on in his office. He hadn't come over since the afternoon of the rainstorm, and she found herself wishing he'd come over now and keep her company. She felt nervous. Maybe it was the unseasonable weather, or the disorganized way she'd been living—home two nights, at Will's apartment the night after—and Owen also living in two places. And even besides that, Holly felt she was losing control over something she used to have, or something she used to want—something she'd wanted for so long that she'd stopped being conscious of it until it was missing. It was as if she'd stopped sleeping and hadn't realized it until she started wondering, why am I so tired? Why can't I think straight? Why don't I dream anymore?

*I*t had gotten dark. There were stars appearing, and Holly noticed the half-moon, low in the sky, just before she heard the kitchen door open. When she didn't hear anything else, she went inside and found Owen standing at the sink with his arms bleeding.

"I was running and didn't see the barbed wire," he said without emotion; when he turned around, Holly could see how scared he looked. His T-shirt was ripped and bloody.

"Take off your shirt," she told him. "Sit down."

She phoned Lawson next door; he ran over and looked at Owen and said, "Come over to the clinic, both of you."

There, Holly stood in Lawson's brightly lit examining room and watched him clean Owen's arms and chest. He was efficient and serious, pausing only once to say, "You're all right. None of these cuts are as bad as they look." After he'd bandaged Owen, he gave him aspirin and a tetanus shot and told Holly to phone Owen's doctor in the morning for antibiotics. "What I have isn't going to work unless he grows two more legs," he said.

Holly thanked him, and she and Owen walked slowly down Lawson's steps, through the grass, and into their lighted kitchen.

"I just want to go to bed," Owen said. He crossed the dark hall and went into his bedroom.

Holly knocked on his door ten minutes later. "Do you want anything?" she asked him, coming in. "Are you hungry? You didn't eat much for dinner."

He shook his head. In the light from the hallway Holly could see how pale he was. "When I was running," he said, "it's like all of a sudden I got hit. That's what it felt like. Like I was in a war or something." He pushed his hair off his forehead. "It scared the shit out of me."

Holly sat beside him on the bed. His window was open; the sound of the insects was louder here, in the back of the house, than it was on the porch. "The crickets are going to keep you awake," she said.

"It's the males calling to the females," Owen told her slowly. "They rub a part of one forewing along a row of teeth on the other forewing. The warmer it is outside, the more often they do it."

"Are you studying them in science class?" Holly asked.

"No. We read about them in the sixth grade. We collected some and kept them in an empty aquarium."

"I remember that," Holly said. "You used to talk about them."

"Crystal had us give them names, like each one mattered."

Owen closed his eyes, and Holly sat next to him until he was asleep. It had been years since she'd done that. The last time had been after her father died, when Owen was twelve; he'd woken up, crying, from a dream in which his grandfather had taken him fishing. "Why was that sad?" Holly had asked, and Owen had said, "Because he wasn't there when I turned around."

Now Holly picked up Owen's dirty jeans, which were folded on a chair, and something fell out of the front pocket—a picture of Crystal on their camping trip. Holly put it on Owen's bureau and left the room.

It was almost eleven when she heard Lawson's voice at her screen door. She was in the living room, watching television with the sound turned low.

"I'm on my way home," Lawson said. "I wanted to make sure you were both all right."

"Owen's asleep," Holly told him. She invited him in, and he sat next to her on the couch. The only light in the room was from the television—an old black-and-white movie Holly hadn't been following.

"He'll be sore in the morning, but he'll feel better in a day or two," Lawson said. "Kids heal quickly."

"I'll call the doctor first thing."

Lawson put his feet up on Holly's coffee table. "I've been sitting next door, reading," he told her. "I could have gone home hours ago, but the truth is I'm hiding from Dick. Much as I like him, I miss my privacy."

"I thought you didn't like living alone," Holly said.

"I'd like to live with a woman," Lawson told her. "That's a different thing entirely." He picked up the remote control and turned up the volume slightly. "You look tired," he said. "Try to relax. Maybe it will be easier with me here."

"What do you mean?" Holly said.

"I mean I'll sit here with you for a while," Lawson said sharply. "What do you think I mean?"

"I'm sorry," Holly said, remembering how recently she'd wished he were there to keep her company. "I am tired."

She closed her eyes. Outside, the wind was picking up momentum; a branch fell, and Lawson got up and closed the door. When he sat down again he put his arm around her; a few minutes later she fell asleep.

When she awoke, it was after two, and Lawson had gone. He'd covered her with a blanket and locked the door behind him.

*H*olly and Owen awoke to autumn. A strong wind was bringing in clouds so quickly that the sky kept changing.

"Every fucking part of me hurts," Owen said when he came into the kitchen for breakfast.

"That sentence would say the same thing without the word *fucking*," Holly told him.

"Bullshit," he said. Holly gave him aspirin and called the school, saying he wouldn't be in that day. Then she called the doctor and made an appointment for Owen at ten-thirty. She wasn't scheduled to work, and when Owen went back to bed, she cleaned the kitchen and living room. She was outside, sweeping the walkway, when Owen came out on the porch.

"I could have done that tomorrow," he told her. "Why does the whole house have to be cleaned this second?"

"It just does," Holly said. "I was in the mood to get it done."

"That's a stupid reason," Owen said. He went inside to get dressed, and she drove him to the doctor's office. She sat across the street, in Venus Park, while he was being examined. He didn't want her with him.

"It's bad enough that you're still making me go to a baby doctor," he'd said in the car.

"At least it's a step above an animal doctor," Holly had told him.

She sat on a bench, watching the changing sky and cars going by on the windswept street. A woman was carrying a child in to see the doctor Owen thought he was too old for now. He was probably right, Holly thought, but she hated to think of taking him to the same doctor she went to, because of how old that would make her feel. What was next: Owen having to take *her* to the doctor? And one day picking her up from the Springhaven Retirement Center to buy her dinner and drive her past the house she used to live in? What if nothing happened to her life in between?

She buttoned her sweater and watched two squirrels run up a tree, two birds land together on the power line overhead. In the back of her mind was a song called "Only the Lonely." And before long Holly was planning her own memorial service.

*O*wen came out of the doctor's office with two prescription slips: one for antibiotics and one on which the doctor had written, "Watch where you're going. Don't run after dark."

"He's such an asshole," Owen said in the car. "It's like he thinks I was just running for fun. You'd think he'd figure out . . ."

"What?" Holly said.

"Nothing."

Holly took Owen for lunch at the Neely Brothers Drive-In, on the southern edge of Venus, near the big, new auto-parts store. The drive-in used to be Owen's favorite restaurant, but now he didn't seem particularly happy to be there. They ordered hamburgers and Cokes and watched the carhop walk up to a station wagon. She was a pregnant teenager; Owen said he remembered her from middle school.

"She was a year or two behind me, I think."

"Really?" Holly said.

"I know a couple of girls who have babies," he told Holly. "It's not such a big deal. Their mothers take care of them."

When the carhop brought their food, Owen put ketchup on his fries and ate them one by one before he started on his hamburger.

"Crystal told me about a sixth-grade girl who was pregnant," he said, without looking up from his food. "I think she had an abortion or something."

Holly watched people driving into the parking lot of the auto-parts store, which had been built in the middle of an empty field, now asphalted over.

"I'm mad at Crystal," she told Owen.

"Crystal's none of your business," Owen said. "She didn't do anything to you."

They finished lunch without speaking. Holly watched Owen put down his hamburger without finishing it.

"What do you want to do now?" she asked him.

"I don't care. Go home, I guess."

"What will you do at home?"

"I don't know. Nothing."

Holly started the car and made a right turn onto the highway, away from Venus.

"Well, I feel like driving," she said. "Put on your seat belt. We'll just drive until we feel like turning around."

They drove through Spring Ridge, with its gas station and grocery store and closed-down movie theater, and then west, toward Leigh, past an empty farmhouse with cows standing in the front yard. Out in this direction there were fewer trees, and the fields became less flat. There weren't hills, exactly, but there were long, gradual swells, so that from the top of one you could see the next—yellow fields swaying under the wind, with crows darting down into them.

"Aren't you going over the speed limit?" Owen asked.

"No more than you do. One day in Venus I saw you drive right through a yellow light."

"Thanks for bringing it up now," Owen said.

Holly turned on the radio. She was thinking about how she and Will had driven out here once, back when he was with his wife and it was exciting to be with him, which seemed like years ago. She felt that she and Will were more interesting people back then. They had had secrets together, which made them think they knew each other. How did you really get to know someone, Holly wondered; how did you keep close to someone when all his faults and all your faults were right there, between you, to run into, or trip over, or make you love each other less?

"Stop for a minute," Owen said.

Holly pulled off in front of an abandoned silo. She got out and sat on the hood of the car while Owen walked off into the grass. There was graffiti on the silo—a few FUCK YOU's and UP YOURS, but mostly things like RYAN LOVES JENNIFER.

When Owen came back, zipping up his jeans, Holly pointed to the graffiti and said, "I always wanted somebody to do that for me."

"That's stupid," he said.

"When you feel like that you want a lot of stupid things."

"Are you talking about Dad?" Owen asked defensively.

"No," Holly told him. "Not the way you think, anyway."

She looked out at the field of long grass, which reminded her of a field she and Burke had slept in once—they were drunk, probably, or Burke was, because she could remember staying awake after he was asleep, thinking about what to tell her parents in the morning. She spent her last two years of high school getting into trouble with Burke, and then trying to come up with explanations that sounded reasonable. What made it worse was how hard her parents had tried to believe her.

She and Owen got back in the car. Holly asked if he'd like to drive, and he said no, his arms still hurt. "Don't turn around, though," he said. "Let's keep going."

They drove to Longton, stopping for ice cream, and they stopped in Moline to gas up the car. When they were south of Wichita, Holly asked Owen, "You don't want to visit Grandma and Newlin, do you?"

"No way," Owen said.

They passed harvested fields being plowed under, with egrets following behind the tractors, pecking for bugs. Clouds were shadowing fields in the distance. Along the Chikaskia River she saw hawks perched in branches of the cottonwood trees.

It was dusk by the time they turned around. They stopped in Wellington for dinner, choosing a small restaurant on the main street and sitting next to the window. Across the street, above a liquor store, women were aerobic dancing in a high-ceilinged, lit-up room.

The waitress was a high school girl. "What happened to you?" she asked Owen, after taking his order. He was wearing a T-shirt under his jacket, which he'd taken off; his arms were bandaged.

"I was running," he told her. "I didn't see something."

Outside, a teenager crossed the street with a dog at his heels and waved to a woman sitting behind Holly. "That's my nephew," Holly heard the woman say to her companion. "He'll be in jail before the year's out."

When the waitress brought their dinners—turkey for Holly, a hot roast-beef sandwich for Owen—she gave Owen a Band-Aid covered with red hearts.

"This is for luck," she told him. "Maybe you'll find it in your pocket one day and remember me."

*O*wen fell asleep halfway home, not waking up until they were past Spring Ridge. Then he sat up straight and looked out his window into the darkness.

"What are you thinking about?" Holly asked him.

"Just stuff," he said.

"Like Crystal?"

"Maybe."

"Maybe I was wrong to be mad at her," Holly told him. "I don't dislike her."

"I'm not like you," Owen said. "Just because she doesn't want me around anymore doesn't mean I hate her."

They were outside Venus. There weren't any streetlights yet—just darkness and four lighted houses half a mile away, on County Line Road. One of them was the house Holly had lived in when she was a baby, before her father had bought their house in town. She thought it was the last house she could see, farthest away, but she wasn't sure: Distances at night could fool you.

"You must miss her," Holly said.

"No shit," Owen told her, so quietly and gently that he turned them into nicer words.

18

*S*aturday, at the Hearth, Will was at the front counter and Holly could feel him glaring at her. She'd stayed the night at his apartment—Owen having spent the night at Burke's—and Will had made the mistake of waking her up in the middle of a dream, perhaps about her father; Holly wasn't sure.

"Can't you wait until morning?" she'd snapped at him. "Do you have to have sex the second you want it?"

Now she didn't feel like fixing things.

"Go apologize or forgive him, whichever's the case," Sue-Ellis said on her way to delivering Gene Rollison's lunch; Gene was sitting alone at a booth. "He's being an asshole to work with."

Will was on the phone. Holly heard him say, "If you get the new vacuum cleaner, I get the Dustbuster and the electric broom." He and Evelyn had been arguing about a settlement agreement for the past two weeks.

Holly walked past him and went outside. Overhead, geese were honking, flying south; clouds were moving fast above them. The leaves would be falling soon, followed by snow, Holly thought. She was cold, standing there—the temperature had been dropping all day—and she remembered that Owen had taken only his denim jacket with him to Burke's. Burke wouldn't even notice; he was just as bad, himself. He'd go around all winter in a hooded sweatshirt and a hunting vest.

Inside, Will was still on the phone, and Sue-Ellis was up on a chair, straightening out the top of a venetian blind.

"Holly," Gene said, "what's for dessert today?"

"Cherry pie. It's good. I had it for lunch." She noticed Gene's flimsy cotton jacket and said, "What do men have against warm clothes?"

"We don't get as cold as you do. Testosterone keeps us warm." He was blushing. "It's a scientific fact. I know it sounds silly."

"Well, not silly, exactly," Holly said. "Kind of interesting."

"Gene knows lots of facts," Sue-Ellis said, stepping down from the chair. "He's always saying things that sound like they come out of an encyclopedia."

"Am I that boring?" Gene asked.

"I just don't think words are that important," Sue-Ellis said. "Other things matter more." She squeezed Gene's shoulder and smiled at Holly.

"I'll go get your pie," Holly told Gene, walking out of the dining room so quickly that in the kitchen she ran right into Cleveland.

"Are you and Will still fighting?" he asked her.

"It's none of your business," Holly said. She put a tiny scoop of vanilla ice cream on a deliberately too-small slice of cherry pie.

"The two of you are making me sick. It upsets my stomach when people don't talk to each other."

"It's more likely your food," Holly told him.

"I'll tell you something else," Cleveland said. "You're getting mean."

Holly went out to the dining room. She took Gene his pie, then she walked back into the kitchen, got her purse and coat, and left by the back door, not even slowing down when Cleveland said, "Some of us are overly sensitive."

In her car, driving home along the windy streets, she found herself with tears on her face. Stopped at a red light on the corner of Elm Street, she remembered a day, years ago, when she saw her father cry over something he'd read in the newspaper. She never knew what. After he'd gone to bed—this was when he was already sick, and she was keeping him company while her mother was at a church meeting—she'd read the paper front to back, looking for a clue, combing the obituaries, particularly. She'd never asked what had upset him.

Her father had been hard to reach and hard to understand. He could seem deep-rooted and strange, like something you'd find growing in an ocean bed, but other times he'd seem uncertain and insecure. She'd been afraid to ask him what was in the paper because she'd been afraid to find out what he cared about. She didn't know what she'd find, and maybe she was afraid of what she wouldn't find. Maybe she was afraid she wouldn't find herself.

At home, she washed her face and changed her clothes. She considered calling Will, thinking it might be easier to apologize over the phone, but she was angry at him—not only for being mad at her, but also for leaving his wife and assuming Holly would be waiting for him, and even for not leaving his wife the year before, to prove that he loved Holly, even though she hadn't wanted him to. She ended up calling Owen instead.

"Come and get your warm jacket" was the message she left for him on Burke's answering machine. "It's cold already, and it's going to be colder tonight."

At four-thirty, as planned, she picked up Dick Spearman and they drove out to Marvelle's house for an early vegetarian meal—Marvelle said it was healthier to eat before six. She and Holly had both taken off work; Saturday nights were never busy anyway. "It's not an eating-out night," Will often said.

Franklin Sanders once told them it had to do with Sunday church coming so soon after. "Eating's a sin to more people than you'd think. They get eating mixed up with sex and sex mixed up with sin and sin mixed up with hell. They forget all about forgiveness."

Marvelle was standing in the gravel road leading up to her house, throwing a soft ball for Hoyt to run after and retrieve. The afternoon had turned less windy and more overcast, threatening rain.

"Watch this," Marvelle said as Holly and Dick got out of the car. She took the ball out of Hoyt's mouth and threw it straight up in the air for him to catch on the fly. Then she put the ball in the pocket of her overalls—Holly could hardly believe that's what she'd chosen to wear—and showed Dick around her property. Holly followed, carrying the low-fat gelatin dessert she'd made.

Marvelle walked down the narrow path alongside the garage and opened the side door. "We have company, Curtis," she said, walking in. Curtis was standing in front of the gas heater in Morgan's old camouflage jumpsuit. Behind him was the Triumph on a drop cloth, tools and spare parts all around—everything just as it had been for as long as Holly could remember. The radio was playing rock and roll.

"Hello," Curtis said, without looking up. He picked up a socket wrench and stooped down next to the motorcycle.

"When do you figure to have it running?" Dick asked.

"Any minute now." Curtis frowned at Hoyt, who'd walked in and was panting over his shoulder.

Marvelle called the dog, and Holly and Dick followed her out of the garage and across the gravel clearing into the house. As they left the garage, Holly thought she heard the lock click behind them—not a smart thing to do, she remembered Marvelle saying once, because the gas heater could malfunction. But Holly could hardly blame Curtis, since Marvelle hadn't so much as knocked.

Marvelle opened the front door, and Hoyt ran in ahead of them, skidding on a throw rug. Holly hadn't been out there in weeks. Marvelle's living room was as dark as ever, lit only by a lamp on a corner table, shining down on iridescent feathers and other fly-tying materials.

"That was Morgan's other hobby—besides that motorcycle, I mean. Curtis does it now," Marvelle said when Dick walked over and picked up a hook. She knelt down to pet Hoyt and remained there for a moment, with her face in the dog's fur. Then she stood up and said in better spirits, "I have celery and carrot sticks for appetizers."

The kitchen was brighter, with its white walls and overhead light. Dick stood in front of the window, looking out at the cloudy sky and the woods, the deep ravine.

"It's hard for me to believe how much time has passed," he said. "The sweet gums are starting to change color." He sat down at the table, already set for dinner. He was wearing dark pants and a too-big plaid shirt, and his broad face had become thinner.

Marvelle brought over the appetizers and a pitcher of decaffeinated iced tea, which Holly poured into glasses Marvelle had set out on lilac-colored coasters.

"Here's to Dick soon being his old self," Holly said, raising her glass.

"Thank you," Dick said, "as long as you don't mean old as in years."

"I don't," Holly told him.

"My mother's still around to remind me what old is," Dick said. "Last night on the phone she told me, 'Pray that you don't live to be as old as I am.' "

"I guess she hasn't met anyone yet," Marvelle said.

"Not any men," Dick said. "I feel like telling her, 'Try being a lesbian. That way, you can fall in love at least once before you die.' "

"What do you mean, 'once'?" Marvelle asked. "Didn't she love your father?" She was running her bare foot over Hoyt's back.

"Not especially. I mean, there's love and then there's love."

"When did you start thinking so much about love?" Holly asked him.

"Since Marvelle bought me that stupid book about hearts," Dick said.

Marvelle turned off the overhead light, lit candles, and brought over a vegetarian casserole and spinach salad.

"Would you like me to call Curtis in?" Holly asked.

"Don't bother. He won't come, especially not today," Marvelle said. "Something special is supposed to happen— that's what he said at breakfast."

"Like what?" Dick asked.

"Who knows? He likes keeping secrets, making people feel like they can never know him."

They ate dinner as it began to rain outside; even with the windows closed, Holly could smell wet leaves and moss.

"I have a secret of my own," Dick said, putting down his fork. "I'm moving to Venus. I've made an offer on a house on Cedar Lane, next door to Franklin Sanders."

Holly and Marvelle looked at him.

"I like it here," Dick told them. "I have friends here."

"Yes, you do," Holly said.

"I bet your mother's going to hit the roof," Marvelle said— insensitively, Holly thought, but Holly could see her smiling as she cleared the table, made coffee, and fed Hoyt, giving him leftovers from a container in the refrigerator. Holly and Dick watched her spoon chunks of meat and gravy into a flowered bowl and set the bowl down in front of the dog.

"That looks wonderful," Dick said.

"Don't start that bullshit about meat," Marvelle told him.

They had coffee and Holly's dessert in the living room, Dick and Marvelle sitting on Marvelle's faded couch, Holly in an easy chair that she remembered used to be in the corner.

Holly noticed other changes then, too: The motorcycle poster had been removed from the wall; Morgan's jacket wasn't hanging any longer from a hook on the door; and his mud-caked motorcycle boots, which he'd only worn to hunt with the dogs, were no longer next to the woodstove. The room seemed less crowded. It was hard for Holly to think of Morgan without thinking of him as weighing more than he did—even his belongings had seemed to take up more space than other people's. At the funeral Franklin Sanders had talked about Morgan's heavy heart. Holly remembered Marvelle saying that Morgan had talked about UFO's and traveling to other planets. No wonder, Holly thought; he probably wanted to feel weightless.

Holly and Dick left a little after seven, Marvelle walking with them under the dripping trees out to the car. The rain had stopped; they could hear the radio on in the garage. As Holly drove down the long driveway, she watched Marvelle, in the rearview mirror, move hesitantly toward the garage, then turn around and go back into the house.

Dick had his head back and his eyes closed. Holly turned on the radio and Gussie Dell said, "My daughter, Wendy, is getting married tomorrow. The wedding's even bigger now that everyone she counted on not coming is coming. That includes her second-grade teacher who lives in Idaho and hasn't left the house in fourteen years. It's not that I mind the cost. Living below the poverty level will be good for my character. What I mind is that not everyone at the wedding will be a close friend or relative." There was silence for a moment. "My sister's cancer is back," Gussie said. "She may die or she may not. My guess is she won't. I just wanted to say that publicly."

"Beatrice Keel," Dick said. "Franklin Sanders spoke of her."

"My father and her husband used to bowl together when I was a child," Holly said. "Beatrice gave singing lessons. She was always performing somewhere. She was the star of *South Pacific* one year and danced right off the stage set up in the elementary school gym. I remember I was allowed to shake her hand after the performance."

They were back in Venus; Holly was driving slowly, thinking about how the town had looked twenty-five years ago, and how much easier it had seemed, back then, even to a child, to know who people were. Now, Holly thought, the ways in which people were different from one another didn't seem important or even allowed anymore, unless you were an eccentric, like Gussie Dell, or were part of a group, like Teachers for a Friendlier Planet; that was the only way it was okay to stand out. There were no stars anymore.

She turned onto Cedar Lane and said to Dick, "Let's do something cheerful. Let's see your house."

It was just now growing dark. Holly and Dick pulled up in front of the house and were walking across the wet lawn when they saw a light come on next door at Franklin Sanders's house.

"What does Franklin say to people like Beatrice Keel, when he's not sure they're going to be all right?" Holly asked Dick.

"He reads from the Bible a little. Mainly, he just keeps you company. He told me once that the happiest moment of his life was one Sunday afternoon at church, going into the kitchen for a cup of coffee."

Dick looked through the small octagonal window in what would soon be his front door. "I couldn't think of my own happiest moment," Dick told Holly. "That was eye-opening in itself."

The house was red brick with white shutters, a little larger than Holly's house. She'd driven past it with Marvelle just a few days before, on their way to the pet store to buy Hoyt a new collar. Marvelle had slowed down as they passed the Sanders house, and said happily, "One day I saw Franklin's wife step outside in torn pajamas and yell horrible things at the paperboy."

Holly and Dick walked around to the backyard, Dick showing her the small deck off the kitchen and the oak that shaded it. "That tree sold me on the house," Dick told her. "That, and the fact that this was the only house in Venus for sale."

"Both good reasons," Holly said.

They looked through the bedroom windows before walking back to the car. Holly dropped Dick off at Lawson's and then drove home. She knew she should go to Will's apartment—he was probably home by now, waiting for her to come over and apologize, not knowing she thought he should apologize to her. But she wanted to go home. She felt like waking up by herself in the morning, which was something that used to make her lonely. Now she knew that lonely only described what being alone felt like when it was forced on you, when you were in a hospital, for example, like Beatrice Keel.

Her yard was full of twigs and leaves, brought down earlier by the wind; some of her flowers were still blooming. There hadn't been a hard frost yet. Her stepfather had called the week before, advising Holly to take down her screens, put up her storm windows, and be sure to have her furnace inspected. Six children had died in a fire last winter, he said. "Worrying about dying makes his life worth living," Holly's mother had said to her afterward on the extension phone.

Holly walked up to her house and put her key in the lock; the phone was ringing when she walked in the door.

"Curtis locked himself in the garage and won't answer," Gene said. "I'll pick you up in ten minutes."

19

Holly dialed Marvelle's number and let it ring more than a dozen times; she did that twice before giving up and waiting outside for Gene. She stood in the yard in the same place she had stood five minutes earlier, but now everything seemed less familiar: the night darker, the stars dimmer and farther away.

The day Morgan killed himself was in her mind so vividly that she could see Marvelle's blue blouse and hear Morgan's hunting dogs howling—they'd done that on and off all afternoon and into the night. "Hounds get that way in the spring," Reese Nyles had said—he'd come out to Marvelle's to help her plan the funeral. But it had been hard for Holly to believe the dogs didn't sense something. She had gone out and given them a second dinner in order to shut them up.

Gene drove up in his police car. He put on the lights and siren the moment Holly got in. "Put on your seat belt," he said before speeding out of Venus and turning west onto the highway.

"I was at Marvelle's earlier," Holly said. "I heard Curtis lock the door of the garage. I should have said something."

"Forget about should," Gene told her. "It's a dangerous word."

They didn't talk after that. Holly had never been in a car driven so fast. She remembered her father once saying, "Before I die, I want ten minutes in a souped-up police car."

Gene was driving with both hands on the steering wheel. He passed trucks so quickly Holly could hear the rush of wind, even with the car windows closed. And when he got off the highway and drove over the small Black Creek bridge, the car left the ground for just a second. He slowed down slightly for the gravel road, and braked just before the house came into view. In the headlights Holly saw Marvelle standing in the gravel clearing.

"Do you have an axe or a crowbar?" she said before Gene and Holly were out of the car. Her voice sounded unnatural to Holly, as if she weren't used to speaking. Hoyt was at Marvelle's side.

"Let's not do anything drastic," Gene said. "Not yet. Isn't he often in the garage this late?"

"Not with the door locked. And never without answering. I've knocked and knocked. The radio and lights are on, but they have been all night." Marvelle took a shaky breath.

"Was he upset about something?" Gene asked. "Did anything out of the ordinary happen?"

"Jesus Christ," Marvelle said. "His father committed suicide."

"Well, I know that. I mean, recently."

"Something special was supposed to happen," Marvelle said. "That's what he said this morning. I thought Curtis was just being Curtis."

They were standing on the path in front of the house, between two pots of dead geraniums. "I know what it is," Holly said, suddenly remembering Gussie Dell's program. "Wendy's wedding is tomorrow."

"All right," Gene said. "Now we have some information." He looked toward the garage and then at Marvelle. "I doubt if they are, but do you know if any of the guns are missing?"

"They're not," Marvelle said. "But he could have bought another one."

"I bet he hasn't," Gene said. He walked into the house, holding the door open for Marvelle and Holly. "Look in the medicine cabinet and see if you're missing any pills," he told Marvelle, "tranquilizers or whatever. And if you find any, take one yourself."

Waiting for Marvelle to return from the bathroom, Gene looked at Curtis's fly-tying materials—peacock feathers, horse hair, silver hooks. He picked up a yellow fly. "He's good at this," he said to Holly.

Marvelle came into the room holding a bottle of Tylenol. "There's less of these, I think."

"We can probably eliminate that as a worry," Gene said.

They went back outside. The moon had come up—bright and three quarters full; Holly could see halfway into the open field she and Marvelle so often walked through. Gene, with Marvelle and Holly right behind him, went up to the side door of the garage and knocked.

"Curtis," he said loudly, "would you just let your mother know you're all right?"

There was no answer.

The radio was playing a Grateful Dead song Holly remembered from the seventh grade. She looked at the door and at the narrow strip of light around it. Hoyt was right there with them, practically standing on their feet; it was impossible to move without bumping into him. Holly was so tense her back hurt.

Gene knocked again, more loudly. "Curtis," he said, "we understand you're upset and don't want to come out. Just let us know you're okay."

Holly took Marvelle's cold hand. Holly could feel her trembling, and her own hands were shaking. She was taking deep breaths, to steady herself. When she exhaled, she could see her breath. She thought she should get Marvelle a heavier coat, or a blanket.

Then, from inside the garage, came a sound like a click, followed by the ordinary sound of footsteps. A second later they heard the big overhead door opening.

In a single-file line—like mice in a cartoon, Holly thought later—she, Marvelle, and Gene hurried from the side door to the overhead door just as Curtis started up the motorcycle and rode it out of the garage. He rode past the three of them, past Gene's car, and all the way down the road. The noise was deafening at first, then loud; then it faded into a distant buzz. Behind them was the empty, brightly lit garage.

"How long was that motorcycle sitting there?" Gene asked.

"That's not the point," Marvelle said.

"I know," Gene told her, "but it's amazing that he got it to run. Morgan never did."

"I'm going to kill him," Marvelle said.

*S*he walked toward the house, and Holly and Gene followed. In the living room, she picked up Curtis's T-shirt from the couch and dropped it on the floor. Then she went into the kitchen and got three beers out of the refrigerator. She sat with Holly and Gene at the table with its nicks and burns and pushed aside a clean, folded pile of Curtis's laundry.

"I'll tell you one thing. Curtis can wash his own clothes from now on."

"I just feel relieved," Holly said.

"Me, too," Marvelle told her. "I feel relieved enough to go after that stupid motorcycle with a baseball bat."

"It's not the motorcycle's fault," Gene said, sitting between them.

"I figured he'd be all right, though," Holly told Marvelle. "I never really believed he'd hurt himself."

"Are you kidding?" Marvelle said. "Since when have you thought anything good could happen to anybody?"

"I don't know why you always say that," Holly said.

"She's just upset with Curtis," Gene told Holly.

"Because I've seen the stupid things you do to keep yourself miserable," Marvelle said to Holly. "You don't do a thing in the world to make yourself or anybody else happy."

There was silence. Holly put down her beer, and Gene got up and turned off the overhead light.

"Let's try to relax," he told the women. "See the trees in the moonlight? Don't they make you feel calmer?"

"I feel calm," Marvelle told him.

"You do not," Holly said, beginning to cry.

"Stop that," Marvelle said. "You're not made of glass. It's not going to kill you to hear the truth once in a while."

Marvelle went to the refrigerator and got herself another beer. Then she stood next to the window. "Watch Curtis stay out all night," she said. "That's what men do. Give you five minutes of peace before they make you worry again."

"Not all men," Gene said.

"I want to be happy as much as anyone does," Holly told Marvelle. "It's not like I like being unhappy."

"You love being unhappy," Marvelle told her.

"I'm just used to being unhappy," Holly said.

They were quiet. Holly blew her nose, and Marvelle looked out at the trees. Then they heard a far-off buzz, growing louder. They heard Curtis, on the motorcycle, roar up the gravel road and skid to a stop.

"You wouldn't believe how well I got that thing to run," he called out when he stomped into the house in his heavy boots. He came into the kitchen and turned on the light, his face cheerful, his long hair tangled. He was wearing the leather jacket Holly knew had belonged to his father. He got himself a beer.

"Okay," he said to his mother. "I'm sorry."

Marvelle had a look on her face Holly had seen once before, when Hoyt, after eating a turkey she had left on the counter, had tried to fit all ninety pounds of himself on her lap.

"Apology accepted," Marvelle said.

*H*olly and Gene drove back to Venus. Neither of them spoke until they crossed the bridge over Black Creek.

"I've been a good friend to Marvelle," Holly said. "I've tried to make her happier."

"You have," Gene said.

"Miserable is an exaggeration," Holly told him. "I'm not miserable, really. That was Marvelle's word."

"I remember."

"Not that I couldn't be happier, but isn't that true for everyone?"

"It is for me," Gene said.

He was driving the speed limit; compared to the ride out there, Holly felt they were hardly moving, hardly even in a car. She had the feeling that she could open her door and put her foot down on the pavement with no more danger than dangling her foot off the back of a canoe. It was like everything was suddenly safer.

"I think Morgan will be all right now," Holly said.

"You mean Curtis," Gene said gently. "You mean Curtis will be all right."

"Curtis. Right. I guess I'm still shaken up."

Gene looked at her. He rested his arm on the back of the seat, touching her hair or almost touching it—Holly wasn't sure that he was, or if he was, if it was on purpose.

"I know it's late," he said, "but do you want to come out to my place? I could make you a sandwich, or tea or something."

"I'm not hungry," Holly said immediately. Then she heard the words she'd just said as if somebody else had said them—somebody more cautious and less lonely than she was.

"I mean," she said slowly, "that would be nice."

She kept her face averted from Gene's and focused on the empty highway. They were passing the truck stop, with the semis parked beside it, their motors running and their exhausts visible in the cold night air. Closer to Venus were the harvested fields silvered by the moonlight. Holly felt she was looking at these things without seeing them; her mind was facing inward, somehow. Then Gene got off the highway and they were back in Venus, driving past the Hearth, which was closed and dark. Gene stopped for a red light at the corner.

"I guess you've been working for Will Chaffe a long time now," he said in an unsteady voice. "Maybe too long."

He was watching her. Holly looked at the Hearth's windows and at the sign, which still flickered but was off now—as quiet and neutral as the trees along the street.

"I've been working for him as long as Sue-Ellis has," Holly said defensively.

"I'm not talking about Sue-Ellis," Gene said.

"Maybe you should be."

The light turned green, and Gene didn't move. He put both hands on the steering wheel.

"I don't think I'm what Sue-Ellis is looking for," he told Holly.

He drove past Venus Park and onto Ferrisville Road, then past the high school and into the north part of the county. He and Holly didn't talk or look at each other. Finally Holly could see his mobile home in the distance; he'd left his outside light on. He parked the police car behind his own car and surprised her by coming around to her side to open her door.

"I didn't know you were such a gentleman," she told him.

"I know you didn't," Gene said. He unlocked and opened the door of his trailer and turned on the light; he helped Holly off with her coat.

"What would you like to drink?" he asked. "I have tea, coffee, hot chocolate, and some kind of wine, I think."

"Wine," Holly said.

She stood on the other side of the counter and watched him move around the small kitchen. He'd taken off his shoes at the door. He got a bottle of wine out of the refrigerator and caught her looking at him; he smiled and turned away, getting out two glasses from a cupboard.

It was after eleven. Holly opened the door and looked out into the cold night. Gene had positioned his trailer so that it faced not the road but the fields behind it. In the moonlight she could see a wooden shed and beside it a neat stack of wood.

Gene walked over to her. "You should hear the crows late in the afternoon," he said. "They fly into an oak tree at the back of my property. You should hear the racket they make."

The furnace came on, dimming the kitchen light and making the floor vibrate.

"Doesn't that wake you up at night?" Holly asked, turning toward him.

He was standing so close that she could see a frayed place on the collar of his shirt. Without wondering why, without wondering if she should or shouldn't, she reached up and touched it, and Gene put his arms around her. She could feel him breathing and hear his heart beating. She put her arms around him and her face against his shoulder; then she found herself touching the back of his neck and his light hair and remembered Will saying, not very long ago, "You don't touch me anymore as though you love me."

They kissed, and to Holly it was the kind of kiss she'd imagined when she was twelve, before she'd kissed a boy, and again, years later, more urgently, because she was afraid it might never happen: The point at which their lips met became the center of everything—the oxygen they were breathing, the objects in the room, the dark fields outside the open door. Everything seemed to spin around them like planets orbiting the sun.

Afterward Gene closed the door and said, "I've been paying attention to you for longer than you know."

Holly listened to a car speeding past on Ferrisville Road, and to the distant sound of a train. She remembered her mother once saying, "You think too much, honey. You need to sit still more often." The furnace started up again and Holly felt the trailer vibrate.

"I think I know for how long," she said.

At midnight, their wine unopened—they'd moved to Gene's couch and held each other, hardly even talking— Gene drove Holly home.

"We'll get this settled," he told her in the car. "We'll only be disappointing people we would have disappointed anyway."

"That doesn't make it easier," Holly said.

She was holding Gene's hand as they drove down Ferrisville Road, the darkness in the car and on either side of the highway something she could almost feel, as if there were a dimension to things she hadn't been aware of until now. She was wondering what her life must have been like an hour ago, and all the hours, days, and years before that.

*O*wen was home. His car was in front of the house, and lights were on in the living room. "He was supposed to stay at his dad's until tomorrow," Holly told Gene. "He does this a lot lately—just comes back when he feels like it." She started to open the door, then closed it, then opened it again.

"I'll be just twelve miles away," Gene said.

Inside, Owen was in his bedroom with the light off, lying on his bedspread and still in his clothes.

"What are you doing?" Holly asked him.

"Looking out the window," he said.

She looked out his open curtains. She could see the pecan tree in the moonlight, and behind it the outline of the cottonwood trees along the ditch. There was nothing else to see—just his own thoughts and feelings, she imagined, taking shape like movies in the dark room. She sat on the bed, next to him, and touched the side of his face the way she used to when he was a child—the way she hadn't in nine or ten years, afraid he'd get angry and pull away.

"I was staying awake until you got home," Owen told his mother.

20

olly planned to tell Will the next afternoon, after she finished working the Sunday lunch shift, and to tell Marvelle as soon as Will knew. That seemed the fairest way, and would make sense—they were all too busy to talk sooner because Sue-Ellis had called in sick. But an hour later, when the Hearth was full of people, Sue-Ellis walked in through the back door and cornered Holly in the kitchen, in front of Will, Marvelle, and Cleveland.

"I had a visit from Gene this morning," she said. "He could have learned to love me if it hadn't been for you."

Cleveland said, for days afterward, that it was the quietest moment he could ever remember at the Hearth. "I could hear my stomach churning," he told Holly.

"Well," Marvelle said finally. She was leaning against the ice-cream freezer. "I don't think people can learn to love somebody, Sue-Ellis. Like them, maybe. Depending on the person."

Will walked across the kitchen, opened the back door, and shut it quietly behind him.

"You people," Cleveland said.

Holly could hear the clink of silverware and the sound of voices from the dining room. "I'm sorry," she told Sue-Ellis, "but right now I have seven people waiting for their dinners."

"I feel like smacking you," Sue-Ellis said.

"Go ahead then," Holly told her.

Sue-Ellis unzipped her jacket, looked at Holly, and sat down in a chair. "It's not worth it," she said.

Cleveland dished up Holly's dinners, which Holly put on a tray and carried out to the dining room. Among her customers was an elderly man who'd lived across the street from her when she was a child. "I don't think this is mine, honey," he told Holly when she placed a chicken platter in front of him. "Not unless cows have grown wings."

"You gave his dinner to that man in the red suspenders," Marvelle said, coming up behind her. "Here—he gave it to me."

"What man?" Holly asked.

Marvelle took both dinners and delivered them to their rightful owners. Then she took Holly outside for a minute. "Get hold of yourself," she said. "Nothing's happened that wasn't meant to. And these people still need to eat." She opened the door and pushed Holly back inside. "The two of you took long enough," she said, and smiled.

When the lunch rush was over, Sue-Ellis was still in the kitchen, gloomily drinking coffee. "You ruined my life," she told Holly. "But I shouldn't have said anything in front of Will."

"That's right," Holly said.

"I should have made you say it," Sue-Ellis told her.

Holly was already on her way out. She picked up her purse and got her sweater; she left by the back door and got in her car. She drove to Will's apartment, where she found him outside, looking down at the empty pool.

"Don't bother," he said. "I don't want to hear it."

"Nothing happened until last night," Holly said, and then, "I didn't realize how I felt . . ." She looked down at the cement. "It was a surprise to me, too. I was going to tell you after lunch. I've known for exactly sixteen hours."

"So you've kept track of every minute," Will said, and Holly looked away, at the sliding glass door of his apartment. "Why didn't you tell me you didn't love me?" Will said. "Why didn't you say that the night I left Evelyn?"

"I told you to go home."

"But you were taking off your clothes while you said it."

Holly thought about that. "Well," she said finally, "we were in a motel room."

Will stared at her.

"I was confused," she told him. "I didn't know what I felt. I think I made a mistake by having an affair with you to begin with."

Will turned away from her. "I don't want to see you," he said. "You can work at the Hearth next week, but don't come in after that. Find another job." He took a step away from Holly. "Because I can't be near you," he said, his voice breaking, "not until I stop caring."

There was nothing Holly felt she could say. She walked around the apartment building to her car, and she was hardly aware of driving until she was halfway home. She didn't let herself feel anything until she turned onto her street and saw her house, and Owen's car parked in front. Then she felt guilt, followed by relief, followed by freedom.

Owen was out running. He'd left a note for her on the kitchen table and left his unwashed dishes in the sink. Holly changed clothes and put her uniform on top of the washing machine. She went out her kitchen door and looked at the fields Owen ran through on the path he followed, stopping each time to climb carefully—he'd promised her—over the barbed-wire fence he'd hurt himself on three and a half weeks before.

It was four-thirty, and the days were growing shorter. Egrets, which Holly usually didn't see until evening, were flying into the trees. She even saw a heron swoop down over Spring Ditch. She was seeing things more clearly. She had felt awake like that when her father died, except that afterward she'd been left looking back, to what she remembered; she'd only woken up to the past. Now it was different.

When she walked into the house, it was only the Hearth she missed: Cleveland, Sue-Ellis, even, and especially Will, not as the person he was to her now, but as the person she'd known before she entered—without thinking—his compli-cated life.

21

ick Spearman moved to Venus on a cold, wet weekend in late October. He hired Owen to drive a U-Haul truck back from Council Bluffs; Holly and Marvelle went along to help. The three of them boxed up kitchen items, books, and clothes, and carried the boxes and Dick's furniture out to the truck. Dick supervised, not allowed yet to lift anything heavy himself. Saturday night he took them to Morrison's Cafeteria for dinner and paid for two rooms at a Super 8 across the highway—he and Owen in one room, Holly and Marvelle in one across the hall.

"He snored all night," Owen complained to Holly the next morning as she rode back with him in the truck. Dick and Marvelle were behind them in Dick's Ford Taurus. "It

was worse than staying with Dad when he and Annette—"
He looked at his mother.

"I know what you mean," Holly said.

"Why would anyone want to move to a shit place like
Venus?" Owen said a little later, after Holly had navigated
him through Lincoln, Nebraska. "I can't wait to get out."

"Maybe he doesn't think it's a shit place."

"Then he's stupid," Owen told her.

"If you want to get out of Venus so much," Holly said
carefully, "why don't you plan to go to college, the way you
talked about?"

Owen had his turn signal on; he pulled out into the other
lane. "Maybe I will," he told his mother, and Holly looked
out her side window, smiling at the two elderly heads visible
in the slow-moving car Owen was passing.

They arrived in Venus at four. Lawson helped them unload
in the cold rain, and Dick stood at the front door with tow-
els, wiping off furniture as it was brought in. Franklin Sanders
came over to help Lawson and Owen carry in a sleeper sofa.
A neighbor of Dick's in Council Bluffs had helped them get
it into the truck.

"I'd like that sofa upstairs," Dick said. "Am I asking the
impossible?"

"Just the improbable," Franklin said. He, Owen, and Lawson sat down on the stairs to rest, and Marvelle brought them
Cokes. Outside, the rain suddenly turned into a downpour; she
closed the door so that the entrance hall wouldn't get wet.

"Does the roof over the choir still leak when it rains?" she
asked Franklin.

"Come to church and find out," Franklin said.

*B*y six-thirty the rental truck was empty. Everyone except Franklin, who'd been called home for dinner, and Owen, who'd been picked up by Burke and Annette, was in the kitchen, eating vegetarian pizza.

"I miss sausage even more than I miss pepperoni," Dick said.

"That's because it's worse for you," Lawson said.

He was sitting apart from the others, on the floor, leaning against the refrigerator. He'd been cool to Holly all afternoon; she knew he'd seen Gene at her house enough times to understand what was happening, and he knew she wasn't working at the Hearth. In fact, he'd waved to her once, driving past Dr. Christmas, the spruce-tree farm outside of Ferrisville where she'd started working.

Lawson got up now and helped her collect the trash and carry it out to the garbage cans in the alley. The rain had stopped; the wind was stronger and colder.

"What's new in your life besides the policeman?" he asked her after they crossed the lawn.

"Why can't we just be friends?" Holly said.

"It would help if I understood why you chose him instead of me."

Holly stood in the alley with the garbage-can lid in her hand. She looked at the back of Dick's house and at Marvelle, standing on the deck under the outside light, feeding pizza crust to a stray cat.

"I can't put it into words, exactly," she told Lawson. "It's like one person getting a cold and not another, or like somebody in a plane crash versus a person who took a different plane. Anyway, why should I have to explain it? Why do you expect me to understand something nobody else understands?"

"Okay. Don't be so touchy," Lawson said.

They walked back across the lawn. Holly could see Dick through the lighted window, picking up a heavy box.

"He knows he shouldn't be doing that," she told Lawson.

"That's what you don't understand about men," Lawson said. "Knowing doesn't count for much. We just feel our way along."

"So do we," Holly said.

*H*olly got home at eight, to a message from Gene on her answering machine, saying, "Call me or come over, or both."

The night before, at the Super 8, Holly had talked to him on the phone while Marvelle was in the shower.

"How did it go?" he'd asked her. "Did you lift with your legs instead of your back, the way I showed you?" He was almost as safety conscious as Holly's stepfather.

"Yes," Holly said.

"But were you careful not to make the boxes too heavy? Did you remember to leave the biggest ones for Owen, or for both of you to carry together? Did you let him handle the furniture?"

"No," Holly said. "In fact, I'm in a body cast."

There was silence on Gene's end.

"I'm joking," Holly said.

"Well, it's not funny," Gene told her. "Have you ever seen anyone in a body cast? Do you know that you'd probably never walk normally again?"

"I wasn't really thinking about walking," Holly said suggestively.

"Don't fool yourself," Gene told her. "It would hurt almost as much lying down."

Holly gave up then. "I was very careful," she said, "and I'm not hurt, and you'll have proof of that when I see you tomorrow. I will see you tomorrow, won't I?"

"Of course you will," Gene said. "I'd drive up there tonight if I could."

"Good," Holly said. "Good night."

She hung up the phone, picturing Gene at the other end, sitting in his living room, or maybe in his bedroom, and maybe even naked—she had to imagine the details; she and Gene hadn't slept together yet.

"I don't know what's wrong with me," she told Marvelle later. "I'm nervous. You'd think I'd never gone to bed with a man before."

"Well, that's certainly not true," Marvelle said.

She was sitting in a green chair next to the window, looking out through the open curtains at the wet parking lot.

"How would you feel," Holly asked her, "if you were finally with the one person you wanted to be with?"

"Lucky," Marvelle had said.

*N*ow Holly left a note for Owen in case he came home that night, and she drove out to Gene's trailer. The first frost was expected before morning, she heard on the radio; she thought back to spring and to that week in April before Morgan died, when the forsythia and tulips bloomed, when the woods were sprinkled with white dogwoods.

Holly could think of it now without having it seem overshadowed by Morgan's suicide. In her mind his death had moved back a little and spring had come forward. Would that keep happening year after year, she wondered, until Morgan almost disappeared, or would the memories end up equal to each other? Would she find herself saying, "Spring came and then Morgan died," instead of, "Morgan died that spring"? Did the important things in people's lives always survive the less important, always end up on top, the way they seemed to even in the confused tumbling of Nedra Holman's mind?

Gene was outside, stacking wood, his light hair and brown jacket caught for a second in her headlights as she pulled in and parked. They went inside his trailer; Holly took off her coat while he washed his hands at the kitchen sink.

"I called your house three times this weekend," he said. "I just wanted to hear your voice on the answering machine."

"I was hoping that didn't sound like me," Holly told him, then felt foolish. Why hadn't she said, "I missed you," or "I couldn't wait to see you," or "I hated being away from you"? She sat down at the kitchen counter. In front of her was her phone number on a yellow pad, written in red ink and circled.

"I know it by heart," Gene said, when he saw her looking at it, "but I like having it there. I like seeing it." He dried his hands on a dish towel and reached for her across the counter.

Holly suddenly felt the way she had as a child, when her father would startle her by being affectionate and she'd try not to act pleased, angry about the times he'd disappointed her. It was mainly herself she'd hurt, she thought now; it was like making a fist until your hand ached, or like hiding something you ended up missing more than anyone else did.

She reached for Gene, and they kissed with the counter between them. When he came around to her side she put her hands under his shirt; he took off her sweater, and jeans, and his own jeans, and he pulled her down onto the living room rug. He touched her as she'd imagined him doing in her dreams—in bed at night she'd dreamed of his hands on her, of him holding himself over her, naked, his arms taut, saying her name; now her dreams were shadows.

"Gene," she said, liking the feel of his name in her mouth.

Later they were in his bedroom, at the end of the hall; Holly could see the muscles in his back as he reached for the covers they'd kicked off—the room was colder than the rest of the trailer.

Outside, the wind was loud and made the trailer rock. They made love again—as she'd imagined, too, in her dreams: the covers thrown off once more, both of them more abandoned this time, Gene pulling off the shirt Holly had put on when they'd first come into the cold bedroom; she'd put it on so that Gene could take it off. She wanted him to undress her again, to run his hands over her skin, to let her slowly touch him.

And when he had, and they were finally quiet, listening to the wind moan outside, she was suddenly almost crying. She couldn't say why. Then they slept, and Holly dreamed she'd fallen off a boat in the ocean and washed up safe on shore.

She woke, later, at the sound of the furnace coming on. Gene was asleep, turned toward her with his hand on her arm as if he'd been about to tell her something. Except for the furnace and the wind, it was quieter here than it was at Holly's house; there was less traffic, and there weren't the dogs she sometimes heard barking at Lawson's clinic. She moved closer to Gene, and in his sleep he put his arms around her. Next to her, on the nightstand—as if it were waiting for her—was the picture of herself she'd given him two weeks before.

22

It was a memorial service for Beatrice Keel that brought Marvelle back to church. She died on a Saturday afternoon in November—"as the sky was growing dark, with her hand over her heart like she was saying the Pledge of Allegiance," Gussie Dell said on a special "Neighbor Talk" program, entitled "Sister." There was a private funeral on Tuesday, and Gussie arranged a Saturday memorial service to be held in the church at the same time of day her sister had died.

It was a sunny, cool afternoon, the leaves past their peak of color and mostly fallen. It seemed to Holly that half the county came to the service—relatives, congregation members, and people like Gene and herself, who felt close to Beatrice from hearing Gussie Dell talk so much about her. Dick Spearman said he felt a kinship with Beatrice, both of them having been in the same hospital at the same time.

"This could have been a service for me," he'd said in the car on the way there. He, Gene, Holly, and Marvelle had driven together. "I feel like I've walked a little in her shoes."

"Slippers," Marvelle had said, which was one of the many unfunny jokes she'd made on the way there. She had stopped talking when they reached the church.

People were congregated on the front lawn and under the oak trees. At the top of the steps, Gussie Dell was leaning on Franklin Sanders's arm; Wendy, standing next to her, was wearing a maternity dress. "I thought there was something fishy about that quick wedding," Marvelle whispered to Holly.

Gussie Dell's brother-in-law was standing by himself next to the side door of the church. He was gray-looking and arthritic—nothing like the man Holly had known when she was a child, coming cheerfully into the house on Saturday nights to pick up her father. She walked over to him and touched his jacket. "Do you remember my father, Mr. Keel?" she asked him. "You bowled together. He was Billy Owen."

"Sure I remember him," he told Holly. "He died owing me money."

Inside the church were wreaths of daisies and white roses; sunlight through the stained-glass windows left wavy patterns of light on the floor and on the backs of the church pews. Gussie and her family sat in the first two pews, Beatrice's husband sitting at the end of the second row, next to a small grandchild in a sailor suit.

Holly and Gene, Marvelle and Dick sat halfway back on the left side. All the pews were filled. Latecomers had to stand at the back of the church. During the hymns, Holly heard their voices rise above everyone else's.

Franklin Sanders read from the Bible: "Surely goodness and mercy shall follow us all the days of our lives . . ."; he led them in singing "When They Ring Those Golden Bells"; at 4:37, the precise time Beatrice had died, he asked for a moment of silent prayer and bowed his head.

After the prayer, he said, "I visited Beatrice the day before she died. She wanted to know how my wife had redecorated our living room. 'Blue curtains and a curio cabinet,' I told her, forgetting the new chair and the standing lamps. I remembered those things when I got home and looked at them. In the morning, when I went back to tell her, she was unconscious."

He closed his hymn book. "Let's not leave things for the last minute," he said. "Details you think don't matter probably do."

*I*t was dusk when the service was over. As people filed out of the church, the sky darkening but still bright in the west, Marvelle stayed behind, holding the handkerchief Dick had lent her. "I want to sit here," she told Holly. "I'll meet you all outside in a few minutes." Gene and Dick went to get the car.

Holly stood on the steps and watched Beatrice Keel's husband turn into a shadowy statue next to the church sign anchored in the grass. He wasn't able to leave, it seemed to

Holly. He seemed moored halfway between the church and the street.

The parking lot was lit up with headlights, and the church lights had been turned off. When Holly opened the door it was in the light from the cars, softened through the stained glass, that she saw Franklin and Marvelle standing together, all but touching, his head bent down toward hers as he'd stood with her that day in the cemetery.

Love was less of a mystery than Holly had thought. It wasn't about thought, for one thing, unless you thought about the interests of your heart. She felt it had taken her all her life to catch up with, or grow into her own heart; she hadn't, in a funny way, felt entitled to herself.

She could see that love wasn't a mystery at all; it was just a feeling people had. It was why Marvelle had been drawn back to church; and Owen had kept Crystal's picture; and Holly, closing the door behind her as Gene walked toward her up the steps, walked toward him. It was what people did.

About the Author

The recipient of a 1996 Whiting Writers' Award, JUDY TROY was born in northern Indiana. She has worked as a waitress, a salesclerk, and a bartender. She has taught writing at an alternative high school, Indiana University, and the University of Missouri, and she is now Alumni-Writer-in-Residence at Auburn University. Her collection of stories, *Mourning Doves,* published in 1993, was nominated for a *Los Angeles Times* Book Award. She lives in Auburn, Alabama, with her husband, and her dog, Hardy.

About the Type

This book was set in Bembo, a typeface based on an old-style Roman face that was used for Cardinal Bembo's tract *De Aetna* in 1495. Bembo was cut by Francisco Griffo in the early sixteenth century. The Lanston Monotype Machine Company of Philadelphia brought the well-proportioned letter forms of Bembo to the United States in the 1930s.